Three the HARD WAY

AN ACRO NOVELLA

SYDNEY CROFT

RIPTIDE
PUBLISHING

Riptide Publishing
PO Box 1537
Burnsville, NC 28714
www.riptidepublishing.com

Three the Hard Way
Copyright © 2014 by Sydney Croft

Cover art: L.C. Chase, lcchase.com/design.htm
Editor: Sarah Frantz Lyons
Layout: L.C. Chase, lcchase.com/design.htm

ISBN: 978-1-62649-234-9

First edition
December, 2014

Also available in ebook:
ISBN: 978-1-62649-233-2

Share the
»LOVE»

Three the HARD WAY

AN ACRO NOVELLA

SYDNEY CROFT

RIPTIDE
PUBLISHING

Twenty percent of all proceeds from the sale of *Three the Hard Way* will be donated to the It Gets Better Project.

The It Gets Better Project's mission is to communicate to lesbian, gay, bisexual, and transgender youth around the world that it gets better, and to create and inspire the changes needed to make it better for them. Visit their website for more information and to find out how you can get involved: itgetsbetter.org/pages/about-it-gets-better-project.

To all the Sydney Croft readers, old and new, for giving us a chance to revisit the ACRO gang, and for helping us to give back to an important charity.

TABLE *of* CONTENTS

PROLOGUE

"Hey, Taggart! Check this out!"

Taggart didn't look up from the snare he was securing to a tree. Justice was probably just going to brag about his rock skipping skills anyway. Tag would have told him that he should be practicing setting traps, but Justice's snares and deadfalls were almost as good as Tag's. At ten years old, they could string tripwires, dig pitfalls, and lay ambushes like seasoned soldiers. Mostly, that was cool, but sometimes, secretly, he wished he could do normal stuff, like ride a bike or play video games with other kids. Being raised as survivalists sort of had its ups and downs.

"Tag! Look!"

Taggart finally turned to his best friend. Justice was standing at the edge of the pond, his hand outstretched, reaching for the metal rowboat twenty yards out. The boat, empty of everything but two wooden oars, was cutting through the water, coming at them fast enough to leave a wake.

"So you can attract metal objects," Tag said, thoroughly unimpressed with Justice's showing off. "I can too. And I learned how to control my magnetic gift a year earlier than you did." His mom said he shouldn't tease Justice about that, but Justice always rubbed in the fact that his ability was far more powerful. There was no way Tag could have drawn in the rowboat from that distance.

Justice grinned at him over his shoulder. "But can you *repel* metal?"

Suddenly, the boat came to an abrupt stop, and a second later, it pushed back in the opposite direction, its square stern making the reverse journey a little slower and rougher.

Tag ran over to his friend. "Dude! That's awesome! Now you can fix the monkey bars you bent at school."

A breeze blew Justice's blond bangs into his eyes as he turned around to face Tag. The rowboat, forgotten now, bobbed around in a patch of lily pads. "Are you still mad about that? Seriously?"

"Someone could have seen you." Tag picked up a flat, round rock and skipped it across the pond's smooth surface.

"It was no big deal. I just wanted to see how strong my power is."

That was a load of crap, as Tag's mom would say. Justice was playing the whole thing off as if he'd bent the bars on purpose, but Tag had seen the way Justice had lost control of his emotions when a schoolyard bully had cruelly teased a crying girl near the slide, Two rusty nails and a wing nut had flown across the playground to stick to Justice and the monkey bars had begun to bow inward. Justice hadn't stopped until Tag tackled him.

Still, Tag wasn't going to humiliate his friend, and arguing would only make him mad anyway.

"You just need to be more careful. Our moms will kill us if they find out we're using our powers in public. Worse, they'll homeschool us again."

They'd had to fight for the chance to go to public school because their mothers, fugitives from an evil agency that'd used them as human test subjects, wanted to keep them safe and out of the public eye. But Tag and Justice had finally convinced them that they could keep their powers under control. And mostly, they could.

And sure, there were times when they either weren't careful or when they intentionally pushed the boundaries and did something stupid. But geez, they had these super cool powers they barely had the opportunity to use on the seventy acres of middle-of-nowhere Idaho where they lived.

"Maybe we *should* go back to being homeschooled," Justice said quietly. "We don't fit in with the other kids. And they think our moms are gay."

Yeah, that was a recurring theme. Last month, Tag had punched the captain of the football team for calling their moms lesbos. Everyone seemed to think it was weird for two single women with kids to live next door to each other on property they owned together.

Throw in the fact that their houses were what their moms called "off the grid," and the townspeople figured there was a whole lot of weird going on out here.

"If we ever find a place for people like us," Justice said as he skipped a rock that outdistanced Tag's by three jumps, "we have to go."

"A good place, though, right?" Tag's mom always said that not everyone with a special ability was a good guy, and while Tag didn't know much about why they were living in isolation, he knew it had something to do with a group of evil people with powers.

Justice skipped another stone. "A good place."

Tag thought about that for a moment. He loved their little family, but at times, being different got lonely. Finally, he nodded. "I'll go if you go."

Justice grinned. "We definitely have to go together."

"Pinky swear?"

Shaking his head, Justice reached into his jeans pocket and pulled out his pocketknife. "*Blood* swear."

Blood swear? That was serious stuff. Taggart held out his hand, palm up. "I'm in."

Justice took his hand and put the tip of the blade to the heel of Tag's palm. There was no hesitation, just Justice jabbing the knife into Tag's flesh and slashing all the way to the base of Tag's pinky.

"Ouch." Tag hissed as he watched the thin streak of blood well up in the cut.

"Wuss," Justice teased, and then it was his turn to hiss in pain as he sliced into his own palm.

They stood there next to the pond, the sun glinting through the canopy of trees, and met each other's gaze. Even though they were different in coloring and build, looking into Justice's blue eyes was always like looking into a mirror. They weren't twins, weren't even brothers, not by blood, anyway, but there were times when it felt as if they were two halves of one person.

This was one of those times.

"Ready?" Justice asked, and Tag nodded.

Somewhere in the distance, a coyote yipped, urging them on. They clasped hands, their blood mingling in their palms before dripping down their wrists.

Justice tightened his grip. "We can't go back on this now."

"We won't." Taggart worried a lot about the future, wondering every day if the bad guys were going to find them. But for the first time in years, he felt . . . peace. He and Justice would be together no matter what. "We'll find other people like us, and we'll be safe."

"And we'll do it together."

"Always," Tag said.

Justice squeezed his hand. "Always."

CHAPTER 1

J ustice couldn't ignore the message on his phone if his life depended on it. When his boss demanded he report in, Justice listened.

When his boss was Devlin O'Malley, head of the Agency for Covert Rare Operatives and a goddamned badass agent in his own right? Justice was practically at a full run to get to him ASAP, as Devlin's message had not-so-subtly demanded.

Justice hadn't been called to Devlin's office like this—without any knowledge of why—since he'd been a brand-new agent. Back then, he'd been convinced he was being ushered in to get kicked out of the program he'd been desperate to join since the day he'd discovered its existence.

In actuality, Devlin had summoned him that time to welcome him into the fold—Justice had passed all his qualifiers with flying colors. And he'd continued to be a viable and valuable member of the ACRO team, especially after leading several key points on the major Itor bombing a few months ago.

Devlin had been running the agency since his parents died. He'd helped hundreds of agents with special abilities, much in the same way he'd helped Justice: by taking him into the ACRO company in the Catskills, training him, giving him a family. ACRO also took in some regular human agents too, for a variety of reasons—some of them from Dev's days in the Air Force. ACRO was a formidable organization, and although they'd scored some major victories over the past years, evil was always too plentiful to eradicate fully.

"Go right in—he's waiting. Not patiently," Gigi told him cheerfully. She'd been Devlin's PA for the past couple of years, and she was gorgeous. If you swung that way. Which he didn't. But hell, he could still appreciate beauty. Which meant yeah, he could also appreciate the man who currently sat behind the big mahogany desk . . . and somehow managed to dwarf it. Justice suspected it would've swallowed most men, but Devlin was anything but.

"Hey, Devlin."

"Justice. Sit." Dev motioned to the chairs in front of his desk. Dev was feared, respected, and liked, which were qualities that Justice hadn't associated as ever going together, especially not when they were linked with a leader. He'd learned that Dev encompassed all those qualities—and so many more—when he'd all but dragged himself in here four years earlier, devastated by the loss of his mother, among other things.

Sternly, Dev told him, "I need you to listen to something," then pressed a button and a familiar voice growled out from the computer, *"I need to talk to Justice."*

A chill ran down Justice's spine.

"I'm sorry, sir, but you must have the wrong number."

"Bullshit. He works at ACRO. Where the hell is he? Put him on the phone."

And that's when Justice heard Dev's voice on the recording—he must've been called to intervene in the conversation. *"Who the fuck is this? Because if you need help, you can just fucking ask."*

"I did. I asked. To speak. To Justice."

"He's not here. It's me or nothing. Go."

A pause, and then, *"Fuck. I need his help. Tell him to call Tag. Or better yet, here."* He rattled off coordinates, which Justice put into the special mapping program on his phone.

Taggart. *His* Taggart. Somewhere in . . . Buttfuck, Alaska.

He stared down at the scar that ran from the inside of his palm, all the way to his pinky finger, then rubbed at the scar like that would do something magical, connect him to Tag in some way it hadn't been able to before.

No, in some ways that goddamned scar had driven them further apart. So much for blood oaths.

"Is this the same Taggart you told me about? The one who wouldn't come to ACRO with you?"

Justice nodded numbly. The deaths of their mothers at the hands of men with special powers had set them on opposite paths. Justice had embraced his own powers and joined ACRO to fight against evil, while Tag had cursed his abilities—and everyone else who wielded them.

"You wanna tell me how he got ACRO's number?" Devlin asked.

Justice frowned. "We have a public number."

"For the locals. Who think we're a private security company. And that's not the number your old buddy called." Dev braced his forearms on the desk and leaned forward. "He called the secure line. So how did he get the number?"

Caught in the crosshairs of Dev's intense, dark gaze, Justice squirmed, something he hadn't done since Tag's mom had given him a dress-down for breaking her favorite lamp while wrestling with Tag.

"I don't know," Justice said.

Dev gave a slow nod and leaned back in his chair. "Any idea where Taggart's been?"

"None, sir. Devlin. Sorry." He scrubbed his hand over his face, feeling like he was in some kind of daze. Devlin didn't look angry, just concerned. "I tried his old phone number a few times. More than a few over the first year I came here. I'd hoped he'd keep it on, come to his senses eventually, but one day I called and a woman answered. She had no idea who Tag was or what I was talking about." Tag had given the number up, and Justice remembered sitting there, clutching his phone, and realizing that his last tentative connection with Tag was gone. Not that he couldn't find him if he really tried, of course, with ACRO's resources, and he'd certainly thought about it over the years, but his anger at his one-time best friend always stopped him.

Dev paused for a moment before telling him, "Well, sometimes it takes years for people with special abilities to come to their senses. They're not exactly the most trusting bunch."

He should've trusted me. "Right."

"Right," Devlin echoed, tilting his head like he was assessing Justice for weakness.

Fuck that. "So Taggart needs rescuing," he managed, although his voice sounded raw even to his own ears.

"Are you sure that's Tag? Could it be someone pretending to be him?" When Justice immediately shook his head, Dev put his hand up in an *I'm not done* gesture. "Listen to me— This is your life. You need to make sure that's him, and not someone pretending to be him. I want you to listen again and tell me if he's giving you any kind of hidden message."

"Like he's being held hostage?"

"Exactly. That's how Itor and some of the smaller agencies work. They play on our emotions. They use the people we love, and the people who love us."

Justice snorted at that last part, because Tag had given up on him—and on loving him—four years ago when he'd turned into the world's biggest asshole. But, at Devlin's insistence, Justice listened to the recording four more times, the knife burrowing deeper into his heart each time. "Dev, it's him. And he's scared. He always gets extra assholish when he's scared."

Dev nodded. Steepled his fingers, rocked back in his chair, and asked, "Are you too close to this?"

"Uh, yeah." Justice admitted it easily because come *on*. And Dev was pretty much a human lie detector anyway.

"Want me to send someone else?"

"No one else can handle Tag. Trust me." He sighed, thinking of what a damned stubborn bastard Tag could be—never mind his powers, which Justice understood intimately.

"Any idea what he's been involved in?"

For Dev, interrogation came as easily as breathing. At this point, it was an inescapable trait in all ACRO agents, and sometimes, asking questions in different ways elicited new information. Jolted the memory and shook free intel that could help. But not this time.

"I have no idea, Dev. I tried to bring him to ACRO with me. He refused. I haven't spoken to him since I got here." Justice ran a hand through his hair, fighting the urge to stand up and pace. "If Itor has him, we'll get him back."

"And if he's still free, maybe on the run?"

"I'll get him to come in with me this time. He has to."

"If he refuses again?"

"I'll bring him here against his will." He spoke through gritted teeth—and he meant it.

"Good. He's too valuable to leave in the open like that . . . if he's still a free man."

They both knew Dev was thinking about the mercenary Seducers, the ones Itor had been using recently in an attempt to rebuild by gathering up scattered Itor agents, as well as to bring in new recruits against their will. The merc Seducers Itor used were well trained and only worked for the highest bidder—fucking menaces and Itor's best shot at reorganizing. That's why there were bounties on most merc Seducers' heads.

"So, what, if I can find a rogue Seducer along the way and bring him in along with Tag, it's like a two-for-one special?"

Devlin sighed. "Something like that." And Justice swore he saw just a hint of a smile.

"A perfect way to spent the Christmas holidays—bagging a merc." And Justice meant it because Christmastime was Hell on Earth to begin with. Add to that the fact that Tag might reject him—again—and he had to have one bright spot.

"I just have one question, more for Tag than for you. Why ACRO *now*?"

"That's the million-dollar question, Devlin. And it's exactly what I intend to find out."

CHAPTER 2

The metallic snap of a leg trap clicking into its spring-loaded ready position rang out in the cold Arctic air. Taggart stepped away from his handiwork, covered his tracks, and trudged through several feet of snow to the building hidden thirty yards away in the forest. He was freezing his ass off by the time he shoved open the heavy door, when he got a face full of only slightly *less* cold air that told him he'd neglected the fire.

Wasn't *that* just great. He'd never thought he'd see this godforsaken cabin again, yet here he was, playing Mountain Man and failing the basics. Didn't matter that he owned this shithole; two and a half years ago, he'd traded life in the frigid Alaskan wilderness for the sun in Florida, and he hadn't looked back.

He *never* looked back.

Until now.

But that's what happened when you're kidnapped from your bartending job in the Florida Keys by the same evil agency that had tortured and killed your mother. That had been a little over a year ago. Then a couple of months ago, ACRO had torn Itor apart, allowing him to break free of its grip and run like hell to his old cabin . . . a cabin he'd sworn he'd never come back to.

So yeah, he was doing the hindsight thing with every decision he'd ever agonized over and wondering which ones were wrong turns. At this point, the only decision he *knew* he'd gotten right was parting ways with Justice. There was too much pain between them, too many memories that were still too crystal clear with no dull edges to soften them.

Which was why contacting the man had been the hardest call of his life, made only after finally realizing he had nowhere left to run. This cabin was his last stand, and his choices came down to dying in a hail of bullets or begging Justice for help, because he sure as hell wasn't going to let Itor take him again. So, yeah, crawling back to Justice beat bleeding out in the snow.

Barely.

And didn't it just figure that ACRO had assholes running the switchboard? As if it didn't suck enough to have to reach out to his former best friend and lover, he'd had to listen to some pompous prick tell him he couldn't talk to Justice.

Itor had been full of pompous pricks too.

ACRO isn't Itor, Tag, Justice's voice rang in Tag's memory. *They're different.*

That had been Justice's mantra from the day their mothers had finally told them everything they knew about the two agencies that employed—or enslaved—people with special abilities. The difference, according to Justice, was that Itor used and abused people, while ACRO helped them. They were *different.*

Fuck different. If that phone call was anything to go by, ACRO was run by arrogant fuckwads cut from the same cloth as Itor.

Shivering, he removed his snow gear and piled it next to the couch before making a beeline for the wood stove. The iron door creaked open, revealing a sad pile of dying embers. In the dim light streaming through the tiny bulletproof windows, he grabbed the closest thing that would burn—the slip of paper with ACRO's number—and tossed it on top of the glowing embers. He watched with grim satisfaction as the note went up in flames, the last physical reminder he had of his time at Itor. Just one week before ACRO's attack, he'd nearly been caught while copying a file containing basic Itor intel on ACRO. At the time, he wasn't even sure what he was going to do with the information, but damn, today he'd thanked his lucky stars he had it.

Now he just had to wait and see if his theft paid off, or if calling Justice proved to be a waste of time.

Justice.

Shit.

He shoved a shard of kindling into the wood stove with more force than was necessary. A shower of sparks bounced off his flannel shirt, except the one that started to burn into the fabric. He slammed the stove's door shut and slapped the damned ember onto the scuffed wood floor, where he crushed it with his boot.

Jesus. At this rate, he didn't need to worry about Itor finding him and destroying the cabin; Taggart was going to do that himself.

Something cracked like a gunshot, ripping apart the silence. For a heartbeat, his magnetic ability exploded to life, ready for action, ready to use against . . . the pop of sap exploding in the fire.

Ah, damn, he was losing it. He scrubbed his hand over his face, hating that he was this twitchy, but hating more that his power had reared its ugly head. He hadn't used it since the day he'd escaped Itor, hadn't been tempted even once, so the fact that it had engaged so quickly and easily meant he was far more on edge than he'd thought.

Cursing, he flipped on the lights and strode across the room to the front window to peer out into the rapidly growing darkness. Nothing moved, but he'd know if so much as a coyote tried to approach the cabin. The leg trap he'd set a few minutes ago was just one tiny piece of a larger defense system. He'd also installed an arsenal of nonlethal booby-traps around the perimeter and four lethal measures closer in, all four controlled by a single phone on his counter.

Anyone trying to get to him would be in for a lot of nasty surprises. He just had to hope Justice would know what to look for. He should, since Tag had intentionally rigged the area with the kind of stuff he and Justice had played around with as kids. A fucked-up childhood, sure, but he was alive because of it. Every minute of the endless hours they'd spent practicing with traps had been worth it. So had all the time spent learning to shoot, to disguise themselves, to pickpocket, to track and set alarms—all done in preparation for the day Itor found them.

Turned out that you could never prepare for that.

He was about to fetch a beer from the fridge when the lights flickered. The generator needed more gas. He threw on his snow gear again, and ten minutes later, the generator was happy and he was back inside, trying to thaw himself.

December in Alaska sucked. Oh, it might be a Christmas-lover's wet dream, but Tag hadn't celebrated since his and Justice's mothers died on Christmas night.

The next day, he'd lost Justice too, but to ACRO. And the bitch of it was, Justice had gone willingly. The bastard had left Tag behind and had gone with people who were no different than the sick scumbags at Itor.

"*They're different,*" Justice had insisted for the millionth time. "*They're the good guys.*"

"You stupid fuck," he muttered to the empty air as he grabbed that beer.

Good guys. Seriously? Did Justice think Itor thought of themselves as bad guys? Did the KGB, CIA, Mossad, think they were the bad guys? No fucking way. Everyone thought they were good guys. Hell, Al Qaeda and ISIS thought they were good guys too.

Ian thought he was a good guy.

Ian.

Goddammit, that Itor bastard had no business butting into Taggart's ragey memories of Justice. But then, Ian had been pushy since the day he'd sauntered into Tag's Key West bar, oozing sex and danger, just when Tag'd gotten to the point where Justice wasn't on his mind every minute of every day.

He'd fallen hard for Ian, believing he was a sport-fishing charter boat captain. They'd spent six months fucking, talking, and fucking some more. Tag had told Ian his secrets—well, not about his powers or his mother's time as a captive in a secret superagency, but he'd confided about his fucked-up life after his mom died and Justice left. He'd told Ian the sappiest fucking things about his feelings for Justice. Ian had been understanding. Kind. Loving.

And Tag had fallen for it, not knowing that Ian had been screening him for Itor. Six months to the day that Ian had come into Tag's life, Itor captured him. Took him to a training facility in Japan, where he'd been poked, prodded, blackmailed, tortured, and finally sent to Itor's Madrid base and forced to kill.

Because of Ian.

So now, here he was, once again hiding from Itor, but this time begging help from the organization he had avoided for so long.

Now he just had to wait and wonder who would get here first. ACRO or Itor. And the thing was, he didn't know which would be worse. Especially because, while at Itor, he'd killed two ACRO agents.

So it was entirely possible that, by reaching out to Justice, he'd just signed his own death warrant.

And it could very well come at the hands of his childhood best friend and former lover.

CHAPTER 3

Justice landed the plane forty miles outside of the coordinates for Tag's place at an outpost that let him pay for storage for the week. Then he used the snowmobile he'd brought along to get him a mile out.

From there, based on how Tag's mind had worked, even before that fateful Christmas, he had to snowshoe it. And obviously nothing had changed because, as he'd suspected, it took him a good deal of time to thread through the death traps of doom Tag had laced through the heavy, crusted snow leading up to the metal, domed structure the coordinates indicated was his hideout.

Granted, if you didn't know what you were looking for, you could easily pass this place. It'd been built into the mountainside, blocked in by trees, and it didn't stand out at first or even fifth glance.

After a freezing half an hour of battling his snowshoes, bulky snow gear, and Tag's nonlethal traps—and Tag had definitely been practicing—Justice found the ones that could do far more damage.

Why the hell am I jumping through hoops for this asshole? Isn't it enough that I jumped when he needed me? He faced the dome, took off his glove, and gave Tag's cabin the finger.

And Tag must've been watching because Justice heard a subtle *click*, which meant the traps were shut off for the moment. Justice's breath froze on his skin as he quickly crunched through the snow before the bastard turned them on again—for fun. Then the heavy front door jerked open before he'd put a single, booted foot on the porch, and Justice stilled at his first look at Taggart in four years.

Tag looked exhausted. He was as big as Justice remembered—at six feet six inches, he towered over most and had always made Justice feel tiny in comparison at six one. He was as hot as Justice remembered too, all dark hair and lazy amber eyes, and Justice willed his fucking libido to *sit* and *stay*.

Just because he hadn't gotten laid recently wasn't any reason to lose his shit.

Over Taggart.

His first love. The guy he'd wanted to spend the rest of his motherfucking life with.

The guy who'd promised Justice that he'd wanted nothing more than that as well. But instead of "Thanks for making the trip to come help me even though I'm an asshole," Justice got a dose of Tag's typical bullshit.

"What the fuck took you so long, Justice?" Tag demanded, his breath hanging in the still air.

"Good to see you too, *Tag*."

Tag stared at him in that way he had. For a long moment, it was pure coldness but then . . . then his eyes flickered and yeah, there it was, that electricity between them that'd always been able to override everything else.

Until it hadn't.

Tag swallowed hard, and Justice wondered if he could push him back into the cabin and fuck him on the floor—or the couch or the bed—before ushering him to the plane. "Come on in."

Come in and fuck you against the wall? Not a problem. "I uh . . . look, we need to get back to my plane and get you to ACRO."

Tag gestured to the wall of dark clouds looming to the north. "Can't. Storm's coming."

"Okay, Yeti, thanks for the update. I can fly through storms. And look, nothing to the south," Justice motioned over his shoulder. "So the faster you can shut up and get on the plane . . ."

A low-flying plane zoomed overhead.

"Fuck. Get in here." Tag grabbed him and pulled him inside. Justice went along, one hand instinctively hovering over the sidearm in the specially made pocket of his jacket. Tag slammed the door behind them. "Where did you park?"

Grateful for the warmth in the cabin, Justice peeled off his gloves and bent to remove the snowshoes. "The plane? The nearest settlement. The snowmobile? A mile out, hidden by trees." He started to open the door to check if the plane was still close, since this place was fucking soundproofed, but Tag stopped him.

"Don't."

"Who's after you, Tag? What's so bad that you contacted me—contacted ACRO—after all these years?"

"Don't ask questions, Justice. You always ask too many questions."

"Really?" Justice dropped his pack. Unzipped his jacket and let it fall as Tag watched him. "I guess I feel like questions are the way you get to know things. Like, I'm gonna pretend you asked me questions, like you should've. I'm great, Tag. Nice to hear from you. Awesome the way you endeared yourself to the motherfucking head of ACRO—you know, the place you want to go for help right now?"

Tag stared at him, unblinking. "I didn't say I wanted to go to ACRO. I needed *your* help, Justice. Not ACRO's."

"One and the same," Justice ground out.

"Fuck. When did you turn into such a self-righteous prick?"

"Same time you ditched our promise." Justice held up his hand, the one with the scar from the blood oath, and yeah, maybe he'd been a bit dramatic about it. But fuck it all, Tag had been equally so. Then and now. "You brought me here, opened up all these old wounds—"

"I needed help."

"And had me fly halfway around the world to do what? Drag your ass out of here and drop you . . . where? Into more trouble?" He kicked off his snow pants with jerky movements, heard the rip of stitches when they caught on his damned boots.

"You have no idea what I've been through."

"You're right. But I would've if you'd fucking kept your old phone number in service," Justice pointed out. He hadn't realized how much anger he'd built up inside against Taggart, but that asshole had deserted him, and when they'd needed each other most.

"You were trying to force me into ACRO."

"Right. Because this is so much better." Justice waved his hands around this metal biodome from hell. "I don't care what happened to you or whatever else your protests are. You're coming to ACRO with me."

"Fuck that," Tag snapped. "I called *you*. Not *them*."

Unbelievable. "Do I really have to point out that you *did* call ACRO? Their extremely private number?"

Tag ground his molars loud enough for Justice to hear the scrape of enamel. "I didn't have your number. Seems like ACRO erased your entire existence. So, yeah, I did what I had to do, and it worked. You're here. ACRO can stay the hell out of it."

So. Fucking. Stubborn. "Sorry, man, ACRO knows about you now, and there's no taking *that* bullet out of the chamber."

Tag snorted. "So . . . what? You'll take me in against my will?" But he shifted uneasily.

"I'll tie you up. Gag you if I have to." Justice backed Tag against the wall, but Tag held out strong arms, his hands against Justice's chest, keeping Justice from getting too close. "But you like that, right, Tag? Least, you always did."

"Fuck you," Tag spat out.

Justice looked between them. Tag's hard cock was outlined against his pants, same as Justice's. "You need me to tie you for this? The way you used to want it, so you could pretend it wasn't you wanting me, that I was forcing it all on you? I know you liked that and hell, so did I."

"Go away, Justice. This was a mistake." Tag's hands were still holding him off, but they'd also fisted—Tag's sign of want and need— and fuck, it'd been too long.

"Was it? Or did you call me here on purpose because you missed this? Missed us?"

"No."

Justice smiled at the lie. And this, at least, was as familiar as Tag being a miserable bastard. This zap of electricity that always passed between them had been theirs from their first moments fucking.

Justice leaned in, forcing Tag to bend his arms. He licked the side of Tag's neck, a predator marking his prey. "You still smell the same. Taste the same. But I'm going to check everywhere, just to make sure."

He planted his mouth down on Taggart's, expecting resistance. What he got instead was Tag grabbing his hair, twisting his fingers in it, holding him close.

He was going to get Tag's clothes off, fuck him, and then get him on the plane. Bound, gagged, whatever.

But first, he was going to fuck Taggart, and pray he didn't wake up before it was over.

If this was another dream, he didn't want to know.

This had to be a dream. Or a nightmare. Maybe both.

Four years after losing Justice, Tag's body was reacting as if they were still together and nothing had changed. As if Justice hadn't all but destroyed him.

Clearly, Justice hadn't destroyed his dick because it was all, *I'm so happy to see you!*

Taggart ripped his mouth away, but Justice palmed his face in both hands and held him for his kiss. It was brutal and angry and Tag loved it as much as he hated it.

He caught Justice's bottom lip between his teeth and bit down hard, tasted blood. Justice growled, and Tag moaned as the raw, erotic sound vibrated all the way to his groin. Memories of dozens of past against-the-wall make-out sessions flipped through his mind, a distraction that gave Justice the upper hand. In an instant, Justice wheeled him away from the wall, hooked his leg behind Tag's knees, and took him to the hardwood floor.

His shoulder jammed on impact, and his ribs, fractured during the Itor/ACRO battle a couple of months ago, hurt like fuck, but he forgot all of that as Justice came down on top of him and pinned Tag's thighs between his.

"You dick." Justice ripped open Tag's shirt, sending buttons flying. "I see your impulse control hasn't improved."

No, but Justice's fighting skills had. For some reason that turned him on. Turned him on so much that when Justice fell forward, grinding his erection against Tag's and plunging his tongue inside Tag's mouth, he forgot to fight for a moment. God . . . so . . . good. Didn't feel like they had four years of bad history behind them. And when Justice shifted to rip open Tag's jeans and palm his cock, Tag damned near came the way he had back when they were teens and Justice had touched him for the first time.

Wrenching their mouths apart again, Tag grabbed Justice's wrist. "We're not doing this. I didn't bring you here for— Mother*fucker*!"

His balls felt like they were in a clamp, throbbing in Justice's tight fist. Justice's touch was expert, holding him on the razor's edge of pain but managing to make it erotic, and he wondered what he'd have to do or say to make the guy stop.

Or squeeze just a little harder.

They'd had angry sex before, but this was different. This wasn't about Tag getting wasted and forgetting to help Justice study for his physics exam. This wasn't about Justice flirting with another guy just to get a rise out of Tag. This was about real pain, and they had the real rage to back it up.

"I don't care why you brought me here." Justice's fist twisted, just a little, and Tag hissed. "You knew we had to get this out of the way before anything else."

Yeah, he knew that. He'd known it when he dialed ACRO. "I hate you."

If Tag had said that four years ago, he'd have seen hurt in Justice's baby blues. Now he saw only cynical amusement. "Enough to tell me to stop?"

Justice's hold on his sac released, and the next thing he knew, Justice was fisting his cock instead. Tag damn near swallowed his tongue as his ex-lover's hand slid up and down. It was over and he knew it. Fighting this was stupid, but that didn't mean he couldn't go down swinging.

Falling forward again, Justice pinched Tag's lobe between his teeth. "Well?" he prompted. "Do you hate me enough to tell me to stop?"

Taggart arched into Justice's palm. "I hate you enough to not let you fuck me." He drove his fingers through Justice's short hair and yanked his head back so he could look him in the eye. "No. Fucking."

The only sign that Tag's words had struck their target was Justice's subtle inhale. Tag would never let anyone fuck him if he didn't care about them, and Justice knew that. Never. Hell, he'd only ever bottomed for Justice and Ian. Only Justice and Ian had been inside his body. Inside his heart.

"I mean it, Justice," Tag growled. "You so much as try, and I swear to God, I'll—"

"You'll what? Kill me?" Justice's hand wedged lower inside Tag's open jeans until his finger found Tag's hole. Tag bit back a moan. "You don't have a killer bone in your body."

If you only knew. Tag jammed his fist into Justice's ribs and bore down on a particularly sensitive nerve. "No. Fucking," he repeated.

Justice conceded with a shallow nod. "For now."

No, not for now. For forever.

But before Tag could say that, Justice slid down his body in a quick, agile move and opened his mouth over his cock. Holy shit. His hips came off the floor in a massive surge, seeking more of that wet warmth. Justice took him deep and then began a merciless, punishing suck-lick-swallow rhythm that made Tag's vision go blurry.

But not blurry enough to be able to pretend that it wasn't Justice's blond head bobbing up and down on his dick. No, when he looked down his body at what his ex-lover was doing . . . Holy shit, this was really happening.

Part of him wanted to weep with relief—the rest of him dreaded the regret and self-loathing he'd experience the moment it was over.

Pleasure streaked through him, erasing all that emotionally charged bullshit in his head, and he surrendered to Justice's masterful touch. There was plenty of time to mire himself in a black pit of remorse later.

Justice sucked hard, hollowing out his cheeks, and Tag shouted in ecstasy. He was about to blow—

Abruptly, Justice reared up, tore open his own jeans, and shoved them down with his boxer briefs. His cock sprung out, a beautiful dusky column of flesh that made Tag's mouth water. He licked his lips as he watched Justice crawl up his body and put the head of that gorgeous cock against Tag's lips.

"Open your mouth," Justice said, his voice smoky and commanding, a combination that was impossible to resist. "Suck it."

Taggart gave it to the count of five, just to be stubborn. Then, with as much control as he could muster, he parted his lips and accepted the easy push of Justice's erection into his mouth.

They both moaned. Tag knew every ridge, bump, and vein of Justice's cock, and fuck, this was like coming home. Like four years hadn't passed. Tag left all the anger and hatred behind and began to pleasure Justice eagerly, gripping his jeans-clad ass in one hand, while he wrapped the other around Justice's thick length. His own cock was demanding attention, but the bastard could wait.

Pulling Justice in more, Tag forced him to fall forward and brace himself on his palms as he straddled Tag. The leverage allowed Justice to pump his hips and fuck Tag's mouth the way they both liked it.

Closing his eyes, Tag concentrated on the warmth radiating from Justice, warmth he'd missed for a long time. He'd ached for this . . . but had he ached for the sex, or for Justice?

If the sound of Justice's panting breaths was any indication, he was aching, too. Good. Tag was going to make him ache a little more.

Baring his teeth, he scraped them lightly along Justice's shaft, wringing a hiss of pleasure-pain from him before sucking him deep and repeating it all again. And again.

When he was done punishing Justice—for now—he swallowed hard on his cock, and Justice groaned. "So good. You're the best at that."

Ian had said the same thing, and fuck that thought—Ian and his betrayal had no place in what was going on here, now, with Justice and *his* betrayal.

Tag's cock was straining and his balls were throbbing, and this was enough foreplay. Wrapping his arm around Justice's thigh, he forced him to shift positions. For a moment, Justice withdrew from Tag's mouth, but a couple of seconds later, he was straddling Tag's head again and sinking his wet cock back between Tag's lips. Tag moaned around his shaft as Justice's warm mouth engulfed Tag's erection and sucked it deep.

Tag knew Justice had never liked this position, but he loved it, top or bottom—loved giving and taking pleasure equally—and he lasted approximately ten seconds before his balls tugged tight and his climax blasted through his cock. Justice swallowed, milking Tag hard, and even before the last spasms of Tag's bliss faded away, Justice was also coming, his hot semen splashing into Tag's hungry mouth.

Tag took it all, licking and sucking as Justice did the same, taking every last drop Tag had to give. His pulse pounded in ears as pleasure wracked him, and inside his chest, his heart was knocking painfully against his ribs as if warning him against feeling anything besides lust and anger for this man.

His ticker didn't have to worry. Even now, utterly spent and his body trembling, Tag's mind was filling up with all the reasons why what they had done was a terrible idea. No doubt Justice's thoughts were heading in the same direction.

Groaning, Justice shifted off Tag and rolled to the side, his soft, glistening cock resting against his hard abs just inches away from Tag's face. Four years ago, he'd have loved that. Now, feeling exposed, Tag tucked and buttoned up, but Justice apparently didn't give a rat's ass, just lay there, chest heaving under the red Iron Man sweatshirt he wore. The ratty, threadbare Iron Man sweatshirt Tag had gotten Justice as a gag gift during their first year of college.

"Iron Man, get it?" Tag engaged his power, and a pair of scissors flew off the counter and landed in his palm. "You'll always be attracted to me."

Justice rolled his eyes. "Lame, man. Lame." In a flash of motion, he hooked his arm around Tag's neck and drew him in for a kiss. "I don't need a metal suit to be attracted to you," he murmured. "I'm yours."

Tag snorted out loud.

"You wanna let me in on the joke?" Justice asked.

No, not really. The last thing Tag wanted to do was acknowledge the damned thing, because Justice didn't do anything randomly. Putting on that sweatshirt today had been a deliberate choice. Either he was trying to mess with Tag's head, or he was trying to punch him in the heart.

What a jackass.

"I'm just wondering why you didn't dress for Alaska in the winter. You could have frozen out there—" Tag broke off as Justice tugged up the hem of the sweatshirt to reveal a layer of fleece and a thermal shirt.

"I'm not an idiot." Justice's voice was as rough and raw as what they'd just done on the floor.

Shit. This had been as much a fight as it'd been sex . . . and Tag wasn't sure who'd won.

"Did you hear that?" Justice murmured. "A click—"

The door banged open, and a blast of cold and snow roared into the cabin, bringing with it Tag's second visitor of the day.

The second man he'd ever loved.

The second man who'd ever betrayed him.

CHAPTER 4

Justice looked between Tag and the man who'd just burst in. If the guy was armed, he wasn't concerned about reaching for his weapon. Instead, he waited, framed by blowing snow in the doorway, as he calmly removed his hat and gloves, even as Justice, in one smooth motion, zipped up and swiped his Glock from his pack. As the intruder kicked the door closed, Justice leaped to his feet and trained the weapon at his broad chest.

But that look on Tag's face . . . his eyes . . .

Why the fuck was Tag giving this asshole *his* look? Deep inside, his magnetic power stirred on its own. The set of knives on the counter started to inch toward him. Holy shit, he hadn't lost control of his power in years . . . not since the terrible Christmas when they'd both lost their moms. Their deaths had been devastating . . . and the catalyst for the angry breakup that had sent Justice into an emotional loss of control that resulted in Tag's mom's house nearly being stripped of its siding before he could shut down his gift.

Remembering his ACRO training, he inhaled on a slow count of three and cleared his mind. The knives stopped moving, but not before he saw, out of the corner of his eyes, Tag tense up, his gaze on the blades. Wasn't that just great.

He snarled, "Who the hell is this, Tag?"

"Who the fuck are *you*?" the broad man demanded of Justice, who waited for Tag to say something, to make demands of his own about why this random man was bursting in uninvited.

Justice turned to Tag for a quick second, noting that Tag was still staring at the intruder while he shoved to his feet. He was zipped up but not buttoned, and between that and his torn flannel shirt hanging open on his sweat-coated chest, it was all pretty much announcing *I just got blown.* And then he suddenly snapped to. "Ian, what the fuck are you doing here?"

"Saving your ass," Ian answered, and Justice noted that Ian's tone was much gentler than the one he'd used with him.

Oh, no fucking way, *Ian.* "His ass isn't your concern."

Snorting, Ian clicked out of his snowshoes, and Tag chose that moment to grab a log from the stack next to the wood stove, and throw it at Ian's head.

Ian caught it in a motion that was so fast it blurred.

"Ah fuck. Excedo," Justice muttered. Excedosapiens were among the most versatile of the special agents, with a dominance of either super speed or a super strength, and sometimes mixed with other gifts as well. Even super speed or super strength didn't make them invulnerable, though. Justice wasn't Excedo strong, but he'd learned to hold his own in practice with them. He'd learned ways around their speed and strength.

Especially if they had metal anywhere on—or *in*—their bodies.

Ian gave a smug smile . . . until Tag punched him, catching him in a cross hook to the jaw, yelling, "You son of a bitch. You fucking *bastard*!" and following up with a knee to the gut and an elbow to the back of Ian's pale-blond head, and for a moment, Justice thought the Ian asshole was going down.

But a split-second later, Ian snarled, "Motherfucker," through the blood coating his teeth, and tackled Tag, pinning him to the floor. Justice moved closer, weapon still trained at Ian's head.

"He's Itor," Tag managed. "He was a honey trap. He's the reason they captured me."

Tag had been with Itor? What the fuck?

Guess it explained why ACRO now, though. Check. "You both have some goddamned explaining to do."

"I don't answer to you," Ian growled. "Don't even know who the fuck you are."

"You will," Justice promised Ian—who was still holding Tag down—at the same time the floor shook beneath their feet. In the not-so-distant distance, a loud rumble started, growing louder with each passing second.

"What the fuck?" Ian and Justice asked simultaneously.

"Let me up! Let me up!" Tag yelled urgently, and Ian did. As Justice watched, Tag went around, opening hidden panels in the log walls and pushing buttons. It sounded like a part of the house was . . . shifting. And then there was a boom and then . . .

And then the rumble sounded like a freight train, ready to blow right through the middle of the house.

They all instinctively moved to the center of the cabin—and to each other—their backs touching as they formed a triangle, staring out, waiting for the invisible enemy.

"Avalanche," Tag whispered.

"There goes my fucking snowmobile," Justice bitched.

"It was gone before this," Ian assured him, and Justice narrowed his eyes at the pleasantly assholish way the guy admitted, "It was in my way when I drove mine in, so it met an untimely end."

"Fucker." He turned to face Ian, but Tag put an arm between them.

"Could you argue later?" Tag implored.

Justice threw his hands up. "You mean, after the avalanche kills us?"

"We'll be fine." Taggart made an encompassing gesture. "I bought this cabin from a prepper who designed doomsday shelters for the government. It can take an avalanche." He glared at Ian. "But clearly, I need a new lock."

"No," Ian drawled, "you need to use the existing lock."

Justice chose to focus on other matters. "You *bought* this piece of shit? When?"

"After you left me for ACRO," Tag snapped, as if *he* wasn't the one who'd refused to go with Justice after years of swearing he would. "Used Mom's life insurance and the money I earned on a crab boat. So yeah, Justice, glad you approve of my dream home."

"This is *Justice*?" Ian asked, and Justice almost enjoyed the man's anger. "*The* Justice? He's ACRO?" Ian didn't wait for Tag's answer, looked over his shoulder at Justice. "So you're the asshole who fucked up Tag's head so bad?"

He snarled at Tag and hoped the sound of the knives rattling on the counter was just in his imagination. "You told an *Itor* agent about me?"

"I didn't know he was Itor at the time," Tag growled before turning to Ian. "And you . . . you have no right calling the kettle black. I fucking trusted you. I loved you, and believe me, after Justice, I didn't think that would ever happen."

And then there was total darkness.

The noise, the blackness, the anger . . . All of it took Ian back to that horrible day Itor was attacked in a coordinated ACRO sweep of every major Itor site of operations on the planet, including the Madrid offices that housed Tag. Ian had been close to the compound—close enough to feel the ground shake and smell the scorched metal. He'd prayed to find Tag alive . . . but he hadn't found him at all. He'd prayed Tag had survived, but he'd been unable to search him out immediately, for fear of creating suspicion, or putting Tag in danger.

Ian had been patient, waited for Itor to approach him . . . and they had, because he'd been the one to bring Taggart in originally. Itor had told him in the beginning that Tag would no doubt be one of his most difficult jobs.

They were so right, but not in the way Ian had thought.

And then, to discover Tag alive—to walk in on him in the aftermath of fucking another man, only to find out that man was Justice—well fuck, he'd barely been able to breathe.

Just thinking back on it right now was causing the same reaction, but he couldn't stop his mind from going there, now that he didn't have the distraction of Justice gunning for him.

Now that the seeming rejection—and anger—from Tag to him was still burning a hole in his chest, even as he remained backed up against Taggart, could feel the heat from his body burning through him.

And they were trapped. Together. With Justice.

Yeah, someone certainly had a sense of humor.

Taggart had fucking ruined him. Broken through every single defense he'd built up over the years, and when Itor took him, Ian hadn't known what the hell to do with himself. All he could think of was to find Tag, to explain. Try to get him out of Itor. But after ACRO's attack, Itor's main buildings were dust . . .

He'd had no way of knowing if Tag was dead or alive, and that'd slayed him. The only saving grace was that during better times, Tag had shared enough about the cabin "in bumfuck Alaska" to give him a starting point of where to look. He'd also shared his feelings for Justice, about how his love and anger and hatred for the man were all twisted and gnarled together . . . although he'd left out the bits about ACRO and Justice having some sort of yet-to-be-determined special ability.

It shouldn't have come as any surprise that during Tag's time of need he'd call Justice and not Ian.

Ian had betrayed him. Sold him into the slavery of Itor, even though he'd tried his best to convince them that Taggart wasn't the best candidate for their purposes. He'd told his handler, "He doesn't have the makeup for what you want him to do." And despite the fact that he'd fallen for Tag and hadn't wanted to see the evil empire anywhere near him, he hadn't been lying.

Itor hadn't cared, not then . . . and not now. It was one of the main reasons they'd sent him to retrieve Taggart again.

Tiny round emergency lights recessed into the walls flickered to life, lifting the darkness enough to move around.

"Please tell me you've got an underground tunnel or powered heaters or something," he asked Tag as he kicked out of his boots and wondered if he'd look like an idiot if he left on his snow pants and parka. How did people live in this godforsaken frozen wilderness? His face was *still* numb.

Justice looked at Tag like he was praying the man would say yes to Ian's question. Instead, Tag rolled his eyes. "Yeah, I've got both of those, plus a spaceship to fly us up, up, and away." He finished by muttering, "Assholes," as Ian spotted an indoor bathroom.

Okay, well, that was something.

The rumbling eased, and when it finally stopped, Tag strode over to the fireplace, swiped his fingers over a stone midway up the chimney, and a panel slid open. With a few flips of switches, the outside monitors came on. Two of them, anyway.

Ian was pretty damned impressed with how prepared Tag and his cabin both were. Calm, cool, and collected in the face of a natural disaster. Not so much when facing his past, though, but Ian couldn't exactly blame him.

"Looks like a couple of the cameras are casualties," Tag said. "But the good news is that the avalanche only sideswiped us." He hit a few more switches around the room, and the metal shutters on the windows slid open. The ones in the front were clear, but snow completely obscured the windows in the rear of the house.

"I need to check the damage outside," Tag said, then rounded on Ian. "But first, you gonna tell me what the fuck you're doing here?"

He gestured at Justice. "You wanna tell me what *he's* doing here?"

Glaring at Ian, Justice took a possessive step toward Tag, all hackles raised and ready for a fight. "He called me, dickwad."

"And it's something I shouldn't have done," Tag snapped. Ian smirked, but he didn't have time to get cocky because, in an instant, Tag was in his face again. "Did you bring Itor? Are they waiting for your signal to attack?"

"I'm on the run from them too, Tag."

Tag snorted. "You think I'm going to believe anything you say? You're a Seducer. You're trained to lie."

"He's a fucking Excedo *and* Seducer?" Justice's eyes were wide, a healthy dose of respect and a little edge of *holy motherfucker* in his tone. "Jesus Christ, Tag. How could you be so stupid?"

"He's not stupid," Ian growled, not willing to let the man who'd wrecked Tag do any more damage. "I'm just really goddamned good at my job."

"Yeah." Tag's voice was laced with sarcasm. "You should be so proud."

Ouch. "I'm sorry—"

"Fuck sorry!" Tag yelled. "I spent a year in hell because of you. Do you have any idea what Itor did to me? Do you know what they made me do?"

Ian knew some of it, had done his best to check up on Taggart when he could, but ultimately, as a mercenary and not an actual Itor employee, Ian wasn't high on the chain of command, and access to information had been scarce at best. Not to mention the fact that his variety of jobs meant he was rarely even on the same continent as Tag at any given time.

"I tried to help," he said. "I swear, I didn't want that for you. That's why I'm here. I thought you were dead after the ACRO attack. Itor is starting to pick up the pieces, and when they learned you were alive, they came to me. Told me to locate you. I used their resources to throw them off the track—I couldn't let them know I'd known the entire time where you'd be. I planned other routes so they'd find those and I could keep your locale safe. And I intend to."

"By coming here and letting Itor follow," Justice added.

Ian ignored him. "Tag, I only came here to warn you. To get you someplace safe."

"Fuck this," Justice said. "He's lying, and he probably led Itor to the doorstep." He raised the pistol, leveling it at Ian's chest. "Let's put his carcass out for the wolves."

So much rage and hatred burned in Tag's eyes that, for a moment, Ian was sure he was a dead man. How could Tag trust Justice but not him? Granted, Ian had lied to Tag for six months, but he'd also told the truth. He'd fallen in love with him, and that had never been a lie. Justice, on the other hand, had trashed not only their love, but over twenty years of history between them.

No doubt Justice had his own side of the story, but Ian didn't give a shit about it.

Ian held his breath as Tag looked between him and Justice. With his super speed, he could probably take down Justice before he fired his weapon, but Ian would rather the situation didn't come to that. He was fast, but not fast enough to outrun a bullet if things went south.

An eternity later, Tag shook his head. "I don't know what to believe. Justice, put away the gun. If Ian's telling the truth, he can help." As Justice complied, Tag kicked up the bearskin rug in front of the fireplace to reveal a hidden door. "There's a storm coming. I'm going to check out the supplies in the cellar. You two secret agency pukes can take a hike, for all I care."

Justice shot forward and grabbed Tag's arm, and Ian prepared to deck the fucker. "You can't honestly believe this asshole didn't bring Itor."

"I told you," Tag said, as he jerked out of Justice's grip, "I don't know what to believe."

Justice snorted in disgust. "You always were gullible."

Tag just looked sad, and Ian's heart sank when Tag murmured, "Yeah, I was."

CHAPTER 5

Justice watched Tag disappear down the basement stairs. He slammed the hatch door behind him too, leaving no doubt that he wanted to be left the fuck alone.

He glanced over at Ian. *Guess you can't always get what you want.* "This is going to be a long-assed storm."

"Saw it on the radar on my way in," Ian offered as he looked out the window. "Between the avalanche and the blizzard, we've bought some time before anyone can move out there."

"Anyone? Or Itor?" Justice asked, purposefully murdering any pretense that there could be a second of peace between them.

"Both," Ian shot back. "I have no idea who's after *you*."

"After me?"

"I know—hard to believe that anyone would want to kill a ray of sunshine like yourself, but I'm betting it's not out of the norm."

Justice leveled his pistol at Ian's broad chest again, unsure why he'd bothered to put the weapon away when Tag told him to. He'd seen a lot of Seducers in his time with ACRO—all the agencies like ACRO and Itor employed them—men and women well versed in the art of sex and communication, brainwashing and information gathering.

A man's defenses are down when he's fucking—no two ways around it, was Devlin's favorite saying, and sometimes he didn't mean it in a bad way. Not when he was lecturing Seducers. Ian definitely would've had a thriving career as one of them—he was about Justice's height, broad and built, handsome in a way that screamed sexy. Although Justice wouldn't have gotten gay or bi off him, that was the point: Seducers were tri-sexual—they'd try anything. And in Justice's eyes, that wasn't a compliment.

"How long've you been a Seducer?"

"How long have you been a judgmental prick?" Ian smiled pleasantly.

"Long time now," Justice said easily. "So I'm guessing, long enough that maybe your dick's ready to fall off?"

"You're worried about my dick now, Justice? That's sweet of you."

Jesus, he didn't want to think about Ian's dick or Ian's dick anywhere near Tag's dick or ass or mouth, where it'd no doubt been constantly when they were together. Tag's sexual appetites ran toward the insatiable side, something that he'd definitely welcomed.

Justice took a breath and started. "I'm worried about Tag, same as always. And I can't believe he trusted you. That he still trusts you." So much for controlling the snarl in his voice. Because really, what was supposed to happen here? He and Ian running hand in hand through the snow, becoming BFFs?

No, they were fighting over Tag, and it was winner take all. And Ian was a dangerous man, a dangerous agent, thanks to his Excedo status . . .

Justice kept his weapon aimed directly at Ian's heart, even as Ian squared off, like he thought he could take Justice down before he pulled the trigger—and as Excedo, maybe he could. Hell, maybe that's why Tag had left them in here, hoping they'd kill each other. Or at least one of them. Wouldn't that be convenient, so Tag didn't have to make a decision.

Justice's stomach clenched. Before this, he'd known only that he had to convince Tag to come with him to ACRO. Now it was a matter of choosing between him or this asshole Seducer freak. And judging by the way Tag had looked at Ian, the way Ian had looked back . . . Well fuck, Devlin wasn't going to be happy about these developments at all. Maybe there was another way around this.

"I think you should go. Run away, fast and furious through the snow like a good little Excedo. If you gave a shit about Tag, you'd do that for him."

"I'm sure you'd love for that to happen, Justice, but forget it. Because you fucked him up, big time."

"Right. This is all my fault. I was the one who pretended to love him but really just fucked him right into Itor's hands." Justice forced himself not to see the sudden fresh burst of pain haunt Ian's expression. No, he ignored it, twisted the knife a little deeper. "But you've supposedly left Itor, right? Yet, conveniently, you're still letting them feed you intel about where Tag is. And I'm sure you're not going to say a word to Itor about any of this."

"I'm not."

"Then strip."

"What the fuck for?"

"Let's see if you're wired up or sporting transmitters."

Ian smirked a little. He'd already taken off his hat and gloves and dropped them carelessly on the floor, and now he unzipped his parka and let it fall off his shoulders. There was a thud when it hit the ground—weapons and a sat phone, most likely—and Justice was about to grab for the jacket when Ian peeled off his snow pants and followed up by stripping away two layers of shirts, leaving him only in jeans. Justice forgot what he'd been planning to do just seconds earlier, completely fucking distracted, his heart slamming into his chest at the perfectly chiseled body typical of Excedos.

It's been too long for you . . . should've gotten something before you came here. The angry orgasm with Tag hadn't been enough, not when the sex had been more about power than getting off.

And hell, Justice had asked for Ian to basically get naked. Ian, who was smirking even harder, like he knew what Justice was thinking.

He's probably Speedy Gonzales in bed too. Maybe Tag'd forgotten what fucking a guy who doesn't need to speed through the act was like.

Yeah, and he'd keep telling himself that until he believed it.

"Come on, Justice—come closer and check me out." Ian's words were a taunt. He began to unbutton his jeans and made like he was about to slide them off his hips.

"You really left Itor?" Justice asked, trying to distract him.

Ian paused. "Yes."

He sounded sure, and he looked Justice right in the eyes. But still, something about the initial hesitation of Ian's answer made Justice ask, "You worked exclusively for Itor?"

"Who wants to know?"

"The guy standing in front of you with the gun, asshole."

Ian shrugged a bare, well-muscled shoulder, like none of that mattered. "Why don't you ask your best friend? The one you care so much about."

"Figured you'd like this one-sided story business," Justice muttered. "Maybe you two are perfect for one another. Except for one small fact—he hates you, maybe more than he does me right now."

"So you're ahead by what, a blowjob?"

"It's something." Justice pointed in his face. "It's enough to piss you off, and that's enough to thrill the fuck out of me."

Yeah, Ian would give Justice a thrill. He shoved his jeans midway down his calves, until Justice asked, "What the fuck are you doing?"

Ian looked up at Justice. The habit of going commando had been ingrained in him, so the concession he'd made to come to this eighth ring of freezing hell was to wear silk long johns under his jeans. They fit him like a second skin and made the asshole with the big mouth stop talking for a moment.

Men were so easy. Women, it took way more effort to seduce them. They needed sweet talk and compliments. Men? They just needed to see a hard cock, and it was like a beacon to them.

Justice's tongue was practically hanging out of his mouth. The guy was handsome too, in that all-American boyish charm, save-the-world kind of way. Justice really did believe he could save the world—Ian saw that clearly now.

He also saw that he and Justice could never play on the same team—he doubted there were any gray areas where the guy was concerned. Whereas he'd lived his whole life in the gray.

And why the hell had he suddenly become concerned with the actual enemy, anyway?

He licked the corner of his mouth with his tongue, a light, subtle move as he held out his arms. "I thought you were going to check me over? Feel me for chips and wires."

He kicked out of his jeans and prepared to do the same with his long johns, convinced that Captain America would back off.

Justice did no such thing. And Ian had been wrong before, had miscalculated before, but not like this. Because he was already taking a big chance here. Before he'd left to hunt down Tag, Itor had implanted a chip in the flesh below his shoulder blade, and it was thin and malleable enough not to be discovered under intense scrutiny. But that didn't mean ACRO hadn't come up with ways to detect it.

Still, Ian stood his ground while Justice advanced. Justice held his gun out to the side, but Ian locked gazes with him, and that gaze never broke, even as Justice ran his palm over Ian's chest.

Justice's hand was cool, his touch somehow perfect. Ian fought not to show he was affected, but the long johns hid nothing, and fuck it all, most agents thought Seducers were sluts anyway. Best that Justice underestimate him.

Ian's skin goose bumped when Justice's hands ran up his sides. He'd never make it if Justice actually asked him to pull down his long johns and he had no doubt that Justice would.

"Turn around," Justice told him, his voice low, with just a hint of arousal.

"You're kidding, right? Let you stand behind me holding a gun?"

"I'll take over from here." Tag's voice rose up from behind Ian.

"What?" Justice asked. "You don't want me touching him, Tag?" But his voice wasn't exactly a taunt—there was something in it that made Ian almost growl.

"I don't trust you not to kill him," Tag shot back.

Ian was done with their bickering one-upmanship. Now he wanted to get laid. Or do the laying. "Waiting to get naked," he told them both. "Could one of you just get this over with before I freeze my balls off?"

"Doesn't look like you're cold," Justice leered, but Ian knew it was mainly to piss the hell out of Tag.

And it worked, since Tag elbowed Justice out of the way. "I'm doing this."

"I already checked there," Justice pointed out when Tag ran his hand along Ian's arms. Justice's hand was still on Ian's shoulder and Ian was semisandwiched between the two men who were about to fuck or kill each other.

In Ian's experience, it was always a crapshoot.

Justice looked at him and smirked. At his back, Tag's hands swept along his shoulders, his touch firm and detached, the very opposite of how Tag used to touch him. He held his breath for a second as Tag's fingers skimmed the implant. The thing wasn't detectable to the touch, was even smaller than the microchips used to identify lost pets. But still, Ian didn't breathe again until Tag's hands dropped to his ribs and spine.

A moment later, they moved under the waistband of Ian's long johns, and he sucked in a harsh breath as they snaked lower, along his ass.

"You're going all the way with this?" he murmured to Tag over his shoulder, without breaking Justice's gaze. In response, Tag's hands slid forward, under his balls, his strong hands running along his cock, between his legs, and yes, he was going to go there . . .

"Are you fucking kidding me, Tag?" Justice asked. "You're using this as an excuse to feel up your former lover? The one who fucked you over—in more ways than one."

"Would you rather check him?" Tag antagonized. "Were you having fun with the enemy?" And yeah, really not a good idea for Tag to be pissed when his hands were on Ian's cock. Talk about Ian's life in Tag's hands . . .

Justice's gaze snapped up to meet Tag's. "I'm trained for this."

Tag laughed bitterly. "For feeling up men?"

"No, that's Ian's job," Justice said calmly, and Ian winced internally. Not because he wasn't right, because of course he was, and Ian had never been ashamed of what he did, but hell, he was too used to being the nameless one. The one you could talk about like he was a piece of meat and it didn't matter. They didn't even need him here for this.

"Let go, Taggart," he growled, and Tag complied quickly. He jerked his jeans back up and moved out of the way. Glanced at the fridge because he could really use a beer right now, and Tag was never without half a dozen longnecks.

"Right, Justice—wouldn't want to get in the way of your job as a Big Bad ACRO agent. You know, the job you left me for."

Justice pushed Ian out of the way, and he gladly moved. Swiped a beer from the fridge. These men had their own battle to fight, and Ian would just try to make sure they didn't kill each other.

Or at least, that Tag stayed alive. Justice? Well, he had good hands, but . . .

"The job you ran from like a coward." Justice's voice had deepened, and his body shook like he was ready to implode. "The job that you didn't want to take because you've always been goddamned motherfucking selfish."

With that, he lunged toward Tag.

CHAPTER 6

Tag wheeled away from Justice's attack, but he still caught a glancing blow to the jaw. Jesus, Justice was just as bullheaded as he'd always been. Hell, maybe he was even worse now. ACRO had taken a strong-willed kid and turned him into an immovable rock of a man.

"*You* left me!" He slammed the side of his fist into the cabin wall hard enough to make Ian look up from pretending to be fascinated by the beer he was nursing on the couch. "We could have told ACRO to fuck off and gone somewhere together. Somewhere where no one is a freak with special powers. We could have been normal and happy, like we were in college."

"I wasn't happy," Justice said softly.

Tag stared at him. "Liar."

But even as he said it, he realized Justice was telling the truth. Worse, some small part of him had always known Justice wasn't happy at college. He'd denied it at the time, but there'd been a lingering doubt that had spurred him to make sure Justice was well sexed and taken care of, all in hopes that someday Justice wouldn't leave him for ACRO. He'd sensed his discontentment but only on a level he'd not admitted even to himself.

"I was happy with *you*," Justice said. "But not with our life. I needed more."

"You needed *ACRO*," Tag snarled. "I lost *everything* that day. I lost my family. My home. You." He jabbed his finger at Justice. "And then you took off and left me to deal with the aftermath alone. It was real fucking nice that you handled the funeral arrangements and sale of the properties through an ACRO attorney."

Tag glanced over at Ian, whose interest was now fully engaged as he watched them, his feet kicked up on the wooden crate that doubled as a coffee table. He still wasn't wearing a shirt, and his fly was unbuttoned. He might appear to be one laid-back son of a bitch, but behind those heavy lids, sharp eyes were cataloging everything, and under that firm, tan skin, his body would be coiled and ready for anything.

"You fucking selfish shit." Justice stepped closer to him, his fists clenched at his sides. "I handled everything from a distance because *you* told me to get the hell out of your life. Do you think I didn't lose as much as you did that day? Do you think it was easy to leave you? I begged you to go with me. I fucking got down on my hands and knees and offered you anything you wanted, including my soul, if you'd just join me, and instead, you told me how I was betraying you and our mothers' memories." His tone had degenerated to a serrated growl so full of rage that Tag could practically feel it burn his skin. "How *dare* you talk about betraying them. If you'd listened to me when we graduated from high school, if we'd left *then* for ACRO instead of trying to hide our powers and play at being normal college students, our moms might still be alive. ACRO would have welcomed them too, and they'd have been safe from Itor. They're dead because of *you*, Tag. Their deaths are on you, and—"

With a roar, Tag laid out Justice with a right hook that dropped the other man to the floor. Justice's face was hard as hell, and pain screamed through his hand, but he didn't give a flying fuck. All he knew was that the wounds that had just been opened were too overwhelming to deal with.

Eyes stinging, hand hurting, and his heart cracked wide-open, he grabbed his parka and gloves and stormed out of the cabin and into the frozen wilderness to cool off.

Fuck Justice. Fuck ACRO. And while he was tossing fucks around, fuck Ian. Tag should grab his snowmobile and get out of here now.

Problem was, he could run for the rest of his life, but he would never outrun Justice's words. *They're dead because of you, Tag.*

Four years of denying exactly that was bearing down on him with the force of the earlier avalanche. Four years of hiding from the truth in the isolation of Alaska or in the anonymity of the Florida Keys—before Itor had gotten ahold of him, anyway. But even Itor had given him an excuse to pretend that he wasn't responsible for their mothers' deaths. He'd been busy being tortured or threatened or forced to kill. He hadn't had the time or energy to relive the past and remember how, if he'd only joined ACRO instead of going to college to live a normal life, his mother, and Justice's mother, would still be alive.

So yeah, as snow stung his face and wind froze his eyes, he felt the crush of guilt he'd held off for so long. But unlike the earlier avalanche, this *was* going to bury him.

Well, that had been a hell of a show.

Ian drained half of his beer as he watched Justice peel himself off the floor. The ACRO agent swiped blood from his mouth with the back of his hand, muffling the litany of curses that fell from his swelling lips.

Lips Tag had kissed. A lot. As recently as an hour ago.

"That was pretty harsh, man, blaming Taggart like that."

Justice snarled. "Fuck you."

Ian shrugged. "Just saying. I'll bet he already blames himself for your mothers' deaths as much as you blame him."

And wasn't that interesting? Tag had told Ian that his mother was dead, but he'd said it'd happened in a car wreck with Justice's mom. But then, Ian had believed Justice was a normal dude, and Tag couldn't have just come out and said, "Hey, this evil agency called Itor killed my mom and Justice's mom, and then he ran off to ACRO."

Nope, on the rare occasions where Tag had talked about his past, he'd said Justice had run off to join the military.

Ian would have preferred military. ACRO was populated with assholes. Like Justice.

"I didn't say anything that wasn't the truth." Justice glanced at the door, as if expecting Tag to come back at any moment, but if Justice knew Tag at all—and Ian sure as fuck did after only six months with Tag, so there was no way Justice didn't—he'd know that the guy was, right now, plotting to run far and run fast. "And stay out of it, asshole. It's none of your goddamned business."

"My ass, it's none of my business. I picked up the pieces of him you left behind. For the first time in years, he was happy."

Justice snagged a beer from the fridge, and despite really not liking the jerk, Ian had to admit that he had a fine ass. "That's rich coming from the guy who seduced him as part of a *job*, and then betrayed him to the same agency that killed his mother."

Touché. But this moron didn't know jack shit about the whole story. "It started out that way, I'll admit. But it didn't end that way, asshole. I loved him. I tried to stop Itor from taking him, but they did it before I could warn him." When Justice just snorted, Ian went in for the low blow. He wasn't above hitting someone where it hurt. "Besides, I only got him kidnapped. You accused him of killing your mothers."

Justice glared, a shamed red flush spreading over his cheeks. "I'm not going after him, if that's what you're trying to guilt me into doing."

For Tag's sake, Ian had given Justice the chance to do the right thing. But if Justice's ego was getting in the way, that wasn't Ian's problem.

"Then I will." Ian stood and fisted Justice's ridiculous Iron Man sweatshirt. "Because here's the deal. When all of this is over, I plan to be the one leaving with him. And I won't let anyone hurt him again."

CHAPTER 7

T ag was really fucking glad that it was twenty below out because the cold froze his tears before they could fall. Not that he was crying. His eyes were watering from the sting of the icy air. Big difference.

Son of a fucking bitch!

He heard his words echo through the north Alaskan mountains and realized he'd voiced his thoughts in a shout that, with his luck, was probably going to cause another avalanche.

He looked around in the growing afternoon darkness, happy that the wave of snow that'd broken off the mountain had, for the most part, missed them. The back of the house had been buried under tons of ice, but thanks to the cabin's space-age construction, it didn't appear to have taken any damage. The generator shelter had fared well, although he'd still have to dig out his stores of gasoline. He'd also have to reset most of his traps, but that would mean going back inside for supplies, and that wasn't happening.

He tromped through the snow to the shed where his snowmobile was stored. Thank God the building had been protected by the house. The flow had knocked the small building off-kilter, but hopefully the snowmobile hadn't been damaged. If he took off now, he could make it to the nearest town with gas before the bars shut down.

And what good would that do? Itor would still come after him, and he'd just die drunk and alone in the snow.

But shit, he was dying inside that cabin too.

He wedged the shed door open and went inside, mainly to get out of the wind. The storm was on its way, and it was threatening to be a ballbuster. Which meant hours upon hours of being stuck in a one-bedroom cabin with the two men he hated most in the world.

The two men he'd once loved most in the world.

Fuck.

On the upside, if they couldn't get out, Itor couldn't get in.

Tucking his hands in his parka pockets, he sank down on the snowmobile's seat, which was cold even through his flannel-lined jeans.

He checked his watch: 2:30 p.m. Sunset. God, he missed Florida. He'd really thought he could hack Alaska when he'd first moved here after his mom died. But a long-ass season of crab fishing and then a year of living out here alone like a wild mountain man had changed his mind. Justice had always been comfortable with his own company, but Tag was more social, and he'd needed . . . something.

Things had been good in Florida. Awesome compared to the cold isolation of Alaska. He'd had a decent social life that revolved around the bar where he worked, but he hadn't had a love life. There'd been a few one-night stands, even a couple of month-long flings. But the second things had looked like they might get serious, he backed out of the relationships so fast he left skid marks. He couldn't risk loving someone again.

Until Ian.

He'd tried to back out, but Ian hadn't given up. Now he understood why Ian had been so persistent, but at the time, he'd believed Ian had sincerely cared for him. He'd been seduced with patience and pro-football tickets and *Mystery Science Theater 3000* with homemade popcorn on the couch. Ian had seemed to know all of Tag's favorites. Favorite movies. Favorite books. Favorite food.

And now Tag knew why Ian had known all of that. It had been his *job* to know.

Wind screamed through the trees, and the shed rattled. The door shifted, and Ian stepped inside, cloaked in the last rays of daylight. God, he was good-looking. Short, nearly platinum hair and ice-blue eyes that spoke of strong Nordic genes. Chiseled cheekbones. Perfectly shaped, lying lips.

"It's fucking cold out." His breath formed frost around his mouth as he propped a big shoulder against the wall as if he were a good friend just coming out to the deep freeze to chat. "Should have worn gloves. And a hat. And a fucking snowsuit."

Taggart would have let him freeze, except he was cold too. So as much as he despised using his powers, had even sworn not to use them again, he reached deep into the piece of him he kept locked away and opened himself to his gift. For the span of a heartbeat, he hesitated, knowing that the moment he used his power he'd feel tainted. Evil. But guilt over his mother's death was already a malevolent sludge in his veins, so really, what difference was this going to make?

He let loose, hating the buzz of energy surging through him as his magnetic ability charged the air. A moment later, the shed's north side metal wall began to glow like a stove burner, and heat filled the space. Ruthlessly, Tag shut down his power.

"Shit, man," Ian said softly. "I thought magneto-people could just manipulate metals."

"That's all I could do before Itor lab fucks strapped me to a table and shoved a needle into the part of my brain responsible for my ability." He clenched his fists inside his coat pockets so hard they hurt. "While I was still awake."

But hey, the tradeoff for the agony was that now he could "manipulate the free electrons in metal to create heat," according to the Itor scientists who'd performed the procedure and then forced him to test his new talent. The fuckers.

Ian had the good grace to avert his gaze. Thank God he didn't try to apologize. Tag would've beaten him with one of the skis at the back of the shed. Or better yet, the ax at the front of the shed.

"What about Justice?" Ian asked quietly. "What can he do?"

Tag shrugged. "He can draw and repel metal. Bend it with his mind. His ability was always stronger than mine, though." But where Tag had made an effort to use his power sparingly, Justice had thrown his around like confetti. And if the knives on the counter sliding toward him were any indication, Justice hadn't quite controlled his tendency to attract metal objects when his emotions ran hot.

"Helluva coincidence that two people with similar abilities grew up together," Ian pointed out.

"Itor experimented on our mothers while they were pregnant." He had no idea why he felt the need to bare his soul to the guy who'd done his best to destroy it, but hey, it wasn't as if he had anything to lose. "They were given identical drugs and treatment, but differences in their genetics gave us slightly different powers, I guess."

"How'd they get away from Itor?"

"They escaped. Like mother, like son, I guess," he said bitterly. When Ian said nothing, Tag sighed. "Why did you come out here, anyway?"

"Because you're running," Ian said. "It's what you always do when shit gets real."

Tag bristled. "I do not."

One blond eyebrow cocked. "Remember when I invited you to spend the night at my place for the first time? You went AWOL at work and didn't come back for a week. When you did, you made up excuses not to see me."

Yeah, okay, he'd done that. They'd been dating for about a month, and he'd been starting to let his guard down. Until that point, he'd been content to see Ian whenever Ian showed up at the bar or called to see if Tag wanted to hang out. But about four weeks in, he'd started to look forward to seeing Ian, and he'd ached when the guy wasn't around.

Spending the night would have been a huge step, especially since he'd been on the verge of letting things in bed go places he'd only been with Justice.

Clearing his throat as if it would also clear away all those memories, he said, "That's once."

Ian looked at him like he was a dumbass. "There was the time when you were sick and I brought you soup. I didn't hear from you for days afterward."

Justice had always brought him soup when he was sick in college. Whether it was a hangover or the flu, Justice'd made sure he was comfortable. And yeah, those memories—and others—had often boiled over into his relationship with Ian. He'd only finally let Justice's hold on him go when Itor grabbed him.

"Fuck you."

"See? You're running." Ian stomped his boot, breaking off chunks of snow. "Bet Justice would say the same thing. You run."

"So you came out here to point out my flaws? If you're trying to seduce me, you'd better up your game." Bitterness welled at the reminder that seducing was Ian's job, and he couldn't help but add, "Especially since now I know how you operate."

Pain flickered in Ian's eyes, followed immediately by anger. "Is that how Justice got you to suck his cock?" he shot back. "He upped his game?"

Tag shoved to his feet. "Are you trying to get a rise out of me, or do you really want to know? Because if you want to know, here's the deal. I saw Justice, and I didn't know if I wanted to punch him or kiss him." He glared at Ian. "You, I just want to punch."

Ian snorted, his hot breath turning to vapor in the cold air. "Clearly, since you didn't have *my* cock in your mouth two minutes after seeing me again."

Tag ignored that and sent another blast of his metal-heating power into the far wall. "I was glad Justice was here."

Really glad, considering he'd figured there was a good chance Justice wouldn't come, and then he'd have been screwed. He'd had Itor on his tail for weeks, and he'd thought that he'd be safe here, but the last time he'd gone to town, the locals had told him someone had been nosing around, asking about him.

His only hope for survival had been Justice.

"You're saying you were so grateful he came to your rescue that you blew him?"

Okay, now Ian was starting to piss him off. More, anyway. "Yeah. Basically." Not at all.

Beneath the anger and hurt, despite all the bad blood between them, he'd just been happy to see Justice. And when he'd seen the smoldering heat behind the wall of ice in Justice's eyes, he'd felt his defenses weaken.

The funny thing was that it wasn't the heat that had gone straight to his gut. It was the ice. It was the chilling hardness that hadn't been there four years ago. He could blame ACRO for it—probably would because that was the easy thing to do—but he couldn't stop feeling as though he *had* been at least partially responsible for putting it there.

Then Justice had backed him against the wall and dragged his warm tongue up his throat, and his defenses had taken another hit. Justice had owned him at that moment, and he'd known it.

Justice had to have known it too.

"Good to know," Ian said casually, but there was a note of anger in his voice that Tag hadn't heard before. "Come to Tag's rescue, and get paid with sex."

"Takes balls for a Seducer to criticize sex as currency." Tag struck his mark again, and this time, the hurt remained in Ian's expression. Good. Bastard deserved it.

"I'm sorry." There was an emotional hitch in Ian's voice that Tag had never heard. "It's just . . ." He swallowed. "I've never been jealous before."

Tag thought his eyes might bug out of his head. "Jealous? You have no right to be jealous."

Turning suddenly, Ian banged his fist against the side of the building, and the metallic echo bounced around in the frigid air. This was as angry as Tag had ever seen the normally unflappable man. Tag supposed it could be an act, a Seducer game, but what would Ian have to gain from showing a bit of temper?

Ian tested the strength of the metal with his fist again. "No right to be jealous? You think I don't know that?" Ian wheeled around to face him again. "But what I know and what I feel are two different things, and seeing you with Justice . . . it was like taking a bullet. And you know what the really fucked-up thing about it was? I wanted to kill him, but I knew doing that would hurt you."

"Yeah, you're a real stand-up guy, caring for my feelings like that," Tag muttered, and this time when he saw the pain in Ian's eyes, he actually felt guilty. The worst part of it was that he wanted to grab Ian by his shoulders, haul him up against him, and kiss away the hurt. Maybe if he did that, his own pain would ease.

Except it wouldn't. It hadn't worked with Justice. He'd kissed him. Touched him. Made him come.

And now Tag felt worse than ever.

Somehow, Ian knew. He always did. "Justice shouldn't have said what he did."

Tag closed his eyes, but the darkness behind his lids didn't hide the truth. "Justice was right. It's my fault our mothers are dead."

Ian blew out a long breath. "Knowing what you know now, would you have joined ACRO with Justice to protect your parents?"

Swallowing, Tag opened his eyes. "Yeah. I'd have done anything to keep them safe."

"Then let it go." Ian's voice was low, soothing, and Tag found himself drifting toward him, had to force himself to stop. "You couldn't have known. It wasn't your fault."

"Justice thinks it is. No wonder it was so easy for him to leave me—" He broke off as the horrible truth blindsided him.

Suddenly, Justice leaving Tag all those years ago made sense. Yeah, Justice had always wanted to join ACRO, and maybe he would have eventually, even if Tag's plan for college and normal jobs and a normal life *had* panned out.

But instead, Itor had found them. Killed their mothers. And it was all Tag's fault. Of course Justice had wanted to break all ties with the person responsible—ACRO had just given him the means to do it.

Oh, God. He wanted to throw up.

The guilt over their mothers' deaths had always haunted Taggart, even if he hadn't wanted to acknowledge it, but the idea that Justice thought the same, that he'd actually abandoned Tag because of it . . . Jesus. Tag should have known, should have seen it, but somehow, he'd never let himself go there. That would have meant he'd lost Justice for nothing. Every drop of pain he'd experienced would have been laid at his own feet.

I'm not only responsible for the deaths of our mothers, but I'm responsible for Justice leaving me, too.

"Justice is wrong," Ian insisted. "And if he doesn't come around, he's an idiot."

"Don't," Tag growled. "Justice is a lot of things, but he's not an idiot."

Ian sauntered over, halting within reach. Not long ago, Ian couldn't have been that close without one of them touching the other. "Defending him now, huh?"

Fuck. "No. It's just . . . Fuck, I don't know. I don't know anything. And you . . ."

Ian's hand came up to cup Tag's cheek, and he suddenly lost the ability to speak.

But that, he supposed, was better than losing his mind.

"And me?" Ian said softly, tracing a finger along Tag's jawline. Tag jutted his chin, the stubborn thing. It'd been one of the most endearing things about him, the first trait he'd noticed when he'd first made contact with Tag.

"What about you, Ian?"

"You know everything you need to know. In here." Ian pressed a fist against Tag's chest, over his heart. "I wouldn't be here now if I hadn't fallen for you."

Tag drew in a shaky breath, but his next words were firm. Angry. "You sold me out."

"I did, yes. That was my job." A job he both loved—for bringing him Tag—and hated, for the betrayal he'd been forced to commit.

Tag's eyes narrowed. "And what's to stop you from doing your job again? Why shouldn't I believe Justice is right—that you're either planning to drag me back to Itor or leading them here?"

"I'm not dragging you back anywhere," he promised. "But you do have to take out my chip before it activates."

Tag looked confused. "Chip? We searched you."

"It's called a *micro*chip, Tag. Without a detector, most people would never find it without my help." Ian stared into Tag's eyes, knowing this was most likely his best—and possibly last—shot to make Tag trust him again. "The P-128S chip is practically undetectable if it's not transmitting."

"Even to my magnetic ability?" Tag asked, and Ian's first instinct was to lie, but lies were what had gotten them into this situation in the first place. "No. If you'd turned on your gift while you were searching me, you'd probably have found it."

"Fuck." Tag looked up at the ceiling as if there were a portal to the past up there. "So what's it do, exactly, this microchip?"

"It sends out a homing signal letting Itor know exactly where I am, and that I'm most likely in trouble." Tag narrowed his eyes. "It's not activated at the moment."

"How do you know?"

"I watched Itor set the timer. It's a fail-safe. I've got seventy-six hours left. If I don't contact them within that seventy-six hours, it'll go live." He paused. "At that point, Itor's going to either think I'm in trouble . . . or that I've deserted them."

Tag sighed. "So how do you get rid of it?"

"I don't. If I try to cut it out . . ." He took a deep breath. "If it's exposed to air, it'll self-destruct. Taking me, and everyone within a twenty-foot radius, with it."

Taggart's eyes widened with surprise, and then a true hint of concern. "Jesus, Ian. Is that even possible?"

"Ah . . . yeah. Hello, it's Itor, home of the most powerful evil geniuses in the world." Ian hesitated, and then blurted, "But there's a way you can help me get rid of it."

"Me?"

"I wouldn't ask you . . . I didn't come here for you to do this. But this, showing my belly, my weakness . . . this is the only way I can truly get you to trust me. If the homing signal activates, I'll run, lead Itor away from you and give you a chance to get out of here." He slid out of his parka and shivered as he lifted his T-shirt up over his back to expose his shoulder blade. "Do the honors?"

"What do you want me to do?"

Ian jerked his chin at the heated wall. "Do that to it. Except hotter. Melt it."

Tag took a quick step back, the color draining from his face. "The fuck? Hell no."

"Please, Taggart."

Ian held his breath through a long moment of silence until Tag said, "I can't. Heating a metal wall or bending a fork is one thing. Channeling my powers into a human . . ." He shuddered, and Ian wondered what Itor had done to him.

"You can do it," Ian urged. "Use the powers Itor gave you to give them a big 'fuck you.'"

Tag's entire body trembled. "They tried to make me destroy someone's pacemaker. They twisted and perverted my powers, and they wanted me to murder—"

"Tag." Ian inhaled a ragged breath, his guilt at having put Tag in that kind of position tearing him up. "I'm not Itor, and this won't kill me. It'll *help* me. It'll help all of us."

Tag's throat worked on a swallow. "What makes you think I won't draw it out of your body and let it blow you up?"

"A, it'll kill you too, and I doubt you want to be dead. B, if you wanted to kill me, you'd have done it by now." Ian reached over his shoulder and tapped his back. "I know you can do this."

"You really trust me?"

"With my life. Obviously." Ian turned around and faced the metal wall that was rapidly losing its heated glow.

Tag hesitated, then removed one glove. "Where is it?"

"Use your power to find it."

Tag cursed under his breath, and then murmured, "Ian," before touching his bare skin. "This is going to fucking hurt. A lot."

"That's all right. I deserve it. It's about time you got to cause me pain . . . although being without you nearly killed me anyway," Ian admitted.

Tag rested his forehead on Ian's shoulder. And then Ian felt Tag's lips press against his shoulder blade, several kisses. At first, he told himself that Tag was only doing it to find the chip, but no—Tag's finger sat directly over it, while the kisses rained down around it.

And then the pain began. It didn't start slowly; it instantly became a searing, shooting slice of heat directly at the source. He closed his eyes and grabbed for the nearest object, a snowmobile.

"Concentrate on my kisses, Ian," Tag murmured. He continued mouthing Ian behind his ear, nipping his earlobe, and Ian did as he asked.

Tag was saving his life. This was the only way he could prove to Tag that he wanted to do the same. But hell . . .

He was aware still of Tag's voice, conscious of the fact that he was sinking to his knees because of the pain, the electricity shooting through his body. His head throbbed, his heart beat like it wanted out of his chest . . . and right now, he didn't blame it a bit. *He* wanted out.

"Tag, please, I can't take this . . ."

"You can. You have to. You promised me," Tag urged, without any judgment in his voice. Or maybe that's what Ian told himself in order to cope with the rest of the ordeal.

After who knew how long, Ian came to, kneeling, his hands clutching the grips on the snowmobile on front of him. His fingers were cramped from being wrapped around them for a long time. His head throbbed. And he felt the heat from Tag's body behind him as he pressed his chest to Ian's back, reached to loosen Ian's grip, and helped him ease back against him.

"I guess it worked," he croaked, since he was still alive, despite actually feeling a bit singed.

Tag grunted. "Yeah. It worked."

Ian sagged mentally with relief. "Now we're both wanted men," he whispered. "I'll protect the fuck out of you, Tag. I tried to tell Itor you weren't the right fit. You have to believe me."

Tag turned Ian so they were facing each other. "I— Fuck, I'd be an idiot to believe you again after what you did."

Ian's heart leaped to his throat. "And?"

"I guess I'm an idiot." Tag seized him roughly by the biceps and yanked them both to their feet before pulling him in for a hard, punishing kiss.

Finally, oh, God, finally. Overcome by relief, familiarity, hell, he could admit, it, *love*, he let Tag kiss the ever-loving fuck out of him.

Tag's tongue licked the roof of his mouth, and he shifted closer to rub his cock against Ian's. Ian groaned into his mouth. The residual heat from the metal, combined with the heat from Tag's body, was making him sweat. His hands went to Tag's hips, under his parka, pulling him closer.

Tag's arms wound around him, tight bands, and even though Ian knew they could never hold him in place, he liked to pretend. Tag had always been, hands down, one of the strongest men he'd ever met.

"Please," Tag groaned into his mouth, and Ian knew exactly what he wanted. He slid a hand down the back of Tag's pants, cupped an ass cheek, and squeezed hard. "Please, Ian . . . you know what I want."

Tag gripped his shoulders fiercely as he teased, rubbing Tag's perineum but not coming close to what Tag needed. Finally, he said, "Lube. We need lube," after he broke the kiss, but Tag shook his head.

"Make me come without it. You always could."

"Still can," Ian promised, his hand inching toward Tag's hole.

"Really, Tag?" Justice's voice was cool as it floated up from behind Ian, and Ian and Tag froze. "I know sleeping with the enemy sounds hot as a concept, but you've already been beyond burned—you've been thrown into the fire by him. And you escaped. Barely. And you're so willing to throw it all away again for a quick lay?"

CHAPTER 8

Yeah, it wasn't that Justice hadn't been expecting this, but actually seeing Tag and Ian wrapped around each other—with Tag clearly the aggressor—twisted white hot in Justice's gut.

Tag broke away from Ian, his cheeks burning. "Shut up, Justice."

"Why? " Justice demanded. "Because it's the truth? Because hearing it makes you think with your big head instead of your little one?" He laughed bitterly. "Ian's playing you."

"He's not," Tag protested. "Not this time."

"But you know that he's a merc for hire, yes? One of the most dangerous too?" Justice was making this shit up as he went along, but judging by Tag's nonpoker face, he'd hit gold. "There's a bounty out on his head."

"From ACRO?"

"From ACRO, yes. I'm sure we're not the only ones. He's probably back working with Itor just so they'll provide him protection."

"That's not true," Ian said tightly.

"So what's true, Ian?" Justice demanded. "You're a merc Seducer, right?" Ian glanced at Tag before nodding. "This is really fucking perfect. Tag, move the fuck away from him."

"You're not in charge here."

"You called me in. So, technically, I *am* in charge here, and the second I have a contact signal again, I'll call ACRO for backup, and they'll be here before anyone else. We can do this a lot of ways, but you're not going to be happy with any of them. You only seem to be happy with this one." He pointed at Ian. "And soon, he'll be in jail."

"Ah, I see." Ian smirked. "You're going to round me up and take me in?"

Justice stared at him. "You're pretty happy for a guy who's going to be jailed for treason—or worse." He spoke with equal cheerfulness, because he was going to bring in the Seducer with the bounty on his head and get some goddamned money out of the deal. Maybe a promotion.

What about getting the guy? Because if Tag liked Ian better than him, then Justice definitely wasn't getting the guy at all. And isn't that what he really wanted?

Tag held up his hands—a silent show of surrender? Or maybe he just wanted peace. Good luck with that. "I know what he did. I know what happened to me—trust me, I'll never be able to erase it from my brain. But he came here to find me."

Incredulous, Justice stared. "He came here to take you back to Itor, Tag. Jesus."

"That's not my intention," Ian ground out.

"Right. Forgive me if I don't believe you." Justice shook his head in disgust. "Guess you've made your decision. Hope you have a great life together."

He turned and walked out of the shed, and kept walking, trudging through the snow, even though Tag was calling to him, because fuck this. ACRO might want both of them, but he wouldn't—couldn't—do this himself. Let Devlin send Ender to collect these two assholes. Or they could run off with each other and fuck themselves to death.

He heard a crack—heard Tag shout a warning—and he turned, distracted. Caught his foot in one of Tag's motherfucking traps. Pain screamed through his leg, blurring his vision enough that he could barely make out Ian and Tag coming toward him.

The crack sounded again, and he bent to free himself . . . and then everything went black.

"Justice!"

Taggart battled the wind and deep snow as he struggled to get to Justice, his pocketknife in hand and open, and he didn't even remember digging it from his pocket. But Ian got to Justice first, had the massive tree branch off his unconscious form before Tag got there to release the snare.

Fear snaked through him, joining a massive dump of adrenaline that made his thighs tremble as he crouched next to Justice.

"He's breathing," Ian said as he put two fingers to Justice's pulse. "Strong and steady. Let's get him inside once he's loose."

The wire snare had cut into Justice's calf, and he was bleeding into the snow, but once Tag sliced the rope securing the snare to the tree, the pressure released, and he was able to ease Justice's leg from the trap.

The dumbass. Jesus. If Justice hadn't freaked out and run off in a childlike snit, he would have seen the notch in the tree, the signal they'd devised as children to indicate a nearby trap. If he'd listened to Tag's warning, he wouldn't be injured. If he'd have just . . . Fuck it. There was time to yell at him later. Right now he and Ian had to get Justice out of the cold.

Together, they hauled Justice to the cabin and laid him on the bed. Never taking his eyes off Justice, Ian shrugged out of his coat. "I'm going to need whatever medical supplies you have—"

Tag was halfway to his basement before Ian could finish his sentence. He grabbed two red duffels marked with medical symbols from the supplies at the rear of the basement, hauled them up, and dumped them on the bedroom floor.

Ian had removed Justice's boots and socks and had used his own knife to slice Justice's pants and shirt off. "I checked him over," Ian said. "He's got a leg injury and probable concussion." He put pressure on the calf wound, using one of Tag's clean socks to stem the flow of blood.

Tag had never been affected by the sight of blood, but this was Justice, and as bad as things had gotten between them, he didn't want to see his ex hurt.

He wondered, if the situation was reversed, if Justice would give a shit at all.

Justice was definitely going to be pissed about the clothes, though. Tag hoped he had a spare set in the backpack he'd brought.

Ian looked up at Tag. "I need you to keep pressure on the wound while I gather the supplies I need."

Tag obeyed, not liking how fast the sock was getting soaked. "Why isn't he waking up?"

"He did," Ian said, as he dumped gauze, scissors, alcohol, a suture kit, and a bunch of other stuff on the bed. "While you were in the basement, he looked at me, said I was a dick, and passed out again. Probably a concussion." He pulled one of the two chairs in the room to the end of the bed and gloved up before taking over from Tag.

As Tag let Ian replace the bloody sock with a sterile pad, he glanced through the doorway into the living room, where movement on one of the monitors caught his eye. "Be right back."

Hoping Itor wasn't lurking in the forest, he hurried to the bank of screens, but whatever he'd seen was gone. But wait . . . in another monitor, glowing eyes. He reached over to the remote that kept his lethal trap triggers handy, and waited. He wouldn't activate one until he knew exactly what was out there. It was a principle his mom had drilled into him during target practice: never, *ever* fire a weapon until you've confirmed what you're shooting at.

Holding his breath, he waited.

The eyes shifted, and so did their owner, revealing the outline of something definitely not human. Motherfucking bear. Better than Itor though, so he wasn't about to complain. Besides, in his experience, humans were far more dangerous than any wild animal.

Setting down the remote, he turned away from the monitors and headed back to the bedroom, where Ian had cleaned up Justice's wound and laid out the suture supplies.

"How do you know all this shit?"

Ian threaded the needle. "Went through a phase where I thought I'd make a good doctor. Went to a private combat medical school to see. Turned out that I hate the normal day job thing."

The daily grind was what Tag *liked*. Maybe tending bar wasn't his dream job, but seducing or killing people for a living wasn't up his alley, either.

"So you decided to become a mercenary? Are you wanted by agencies and governments, like Justice said?"

Ian gestured to a package of sterile gauze. "Toss that to me. And yes, it's true. Mostly. Funny thing, being a mercenary with special powers. Specials affiliated with agencies like ACRO and Itor don't get fucked with by governments. Officials don't want the general public to know too much, you know? Agencies handle shit internally and deal with each other the way mobsters deal with other mobsters. But us mercs? We make more money and have more freedom, but we don't have pimps to watch our backs. So everyone fucks with us."

Tag had a feeling the pimp reference was intentional, Ian playing offense before Tag could make the obvious Seducer/prostitute connection.

"So you don't belong to Itor? You . . . hire out your . . ." Body? Services? Fuck, the idea that Ian sold himself like that left Tag both angry and sad.

"Yeah," Ian said roughly. "I do specialty jobs for money. Itor wasn't my first choice of employer, but once they have their claws in you, it's hard to say no. Hell, it can be fatal to say no."

Tag swallowed as a sickening thought popped into his head. "When we were together—"

"No." Ian looked away from tending Justice's wound to peg Tag with serious eyes. "From the first time I kissed you until the day . . ."

"The day Itor took me," Tag finished, not sounding nearly as bitter as he thought he would.

Ian nodded. "I didn't fuck anyone else while we were together, Tag. I was supposed to, a side job in Orlando, but I couldn't."

Tag wanted to say something that would make him a real bastard, something along the lines of, *Gee, you didn't have a problem selling me to Itor, but you had an issue cheating on me*, but the man was helping Justice, something he didn't have to do.

"What about after?" Tag asked, because there was still a little bastard in him. And a whole lot of petty. "How soon did you take another job after I was gone?"

"What, you want to know if the next day I was banging some senator for information?" Ian turned back to what he was doing. "Do you really want to torture yourself this way?"

"You can't do anything Itor didn't already do."

Ian winced. "Oh, I doubt that," he said quietly.

Yeah, Tag doubted it too. Maybe it was time to change the subject. "Is Itor really after you, Ian?"

He exhaled a long, slow breath. "Once they learn that the chip is disabled and that I used their resources to find you instead of turn you in, yeah, they'll be after me."

Tag's gut rolled. Ian had put himself in danger for Tag. Yes, it was Ian's fault that Tag was in this position in the first place, but he'd just put his life on the line to get Tag out of it.

Shit like that went a long way toward making amends . . . as proven by the fact that Tag had nearly gotten down and dirty with Ian in the shed.

It would have been a mistake, just like what had happened between him and Justice earlier.

"Could you go to ACRO?" Tag asked, his brain desperately seeking a way to keep Ian out of Itor's clutches.

Ian snorted. "Do you really think Captain America here is going to let me get anywhere near ACRO? He wants me in chains. And not the fun kind."

"I'll talk to him—"

"Why?"

"Because Itor isn't going to stop coming after you. If you work for ACRO, you'll be safe."

He snorted again. "Are *you* planning to go to ACRO?"

Tag cursed. ACRO might have been an option four years ago, but it wasn't now. He'd killed ACRO agents. They'd probably want him in chains right alongside Ian.

"We aren't talking about me," he said.

"No, we're talking about me going to work at ACRO. Let's say they want me. What do you think they want me for? I'm a Seducer, Tag. I have special skills and training, and I'm good at it. ACRO will want me to fuck people for them. At least as a free agent, I have some control."

Tag's heart broke wide open. "You're an Excedosapien. You have cheetah speed. ACRO can use that. You don't have to go in as a Seducer—"

"Drop it, Tag."

"No," Tag snapped, angry that Ian wasn't making even a token attempt to save himself. And yes, he was fully aware of the irony of trying to get the guy to join an agency he himself had refused to join, but if it was the only way for Ian to survive, it had to happen. "Dammit, Ian, you aren't even trying."

Ian loosed a juicy curse. "I *did* try. Years ago. ACRO rejected me because of my family ties. It's a done deal, so drop it, okay?"

Yeah, like that was going to happen. Tag opened his mouth to tell Ian exactly that, but suddenly, Justice roared in pain or rage or something, and before Tag could react, had kicked out, catching Ian in the temple with a modified roundhouse kick.

"Justice!" Tag tackled him as he sat up in bed, fists swinging and legs flailing.

"Shit!" Ian yelled. "Hold him down!"

As if Tag was just standing around.

As gently as he could, he plastered his body against Justice's and pinned him with a forearm across the throat. It took several tries to gather Justice's wrists in his other hand, especially because Justice was bucking like a rodeo bull, but finally, thank fuck, Ian jabbed a needle in Justice's arm, and within seconds, he settled down.

"That should do it," Ian said. "Crazy bastard."

Tag eased up, and sure enough, Justice just lay there, eyes closed, breathing slowing in a steady rhythm.

Pushing himself over to sit on the edge of the mattress, Tag looked between the two men, and it occurred to him that he was in the most fucked-up situation ever. Two ex-lovers in one room. Both enemies.

Nope, there was no way this could go wrong.

CHAPTER 9

J ustice had no idea how long he was out for, but he woke up, if he could even call it that, woozy and pissed. And pissed that he was woozy.

He blinked, tried to focus. "Where am I?"

"Inside Tag's cabin."

That was Ian's voice. Must be dreaming because last he remembered, he hadn't been inside. He stared up into Ian's face. The guy was handsome, he'd give him that. Handsome . . . and a total prick for trying to fuck Tag when he hadn't been looking.

"You're talking out loud, Justice. Might not realize that."

Ian's voice. Again. Ian's hands, pressing on his bare chest. "Am I naked?"

"Just about," Ian confirmed, sounding way too happy. "Guess it's time to check you for wires." And then Ian's hands slid up his side.

"The fuck?" He tried to push Ian's hands off him—mainly because they felt good and he didn't want to feel good from Ian, and he blurted out that sentiment before he could stop himself.

Ian was obviously trying to hold back a smile. "I'll make sure it hurts more. Promise."

"Fine," he huffed, watched Ian scoot down the mattress to tend to his leg. "Motherfucking Tag's trap. Only got caught because he distracted me."

"Because a tree was getting ready to fall on your head," Tag's voice drifted from somewhere behind Ian.

"A whole tree fell on me?" Justice asked.

"Just a branch."

"Why's my head hurt so much, then?" he complained.

"Was a big branch," Ian said.

"A tree fell on me. I expect more sympathy," Justice told them both.

Ian nodded, his lips pressed together like he was trying not to laugh. "Plenty of sympathy."

He felt a couple of pricks of pain along his ankle and then just some pressure. He drifted in and out of sleep, hearing Ian murmuring directions to Tag, and occasionally he'd hear things like, "mild concussion" and "needs antibiotics," and "he'll be okay, right?"

That last one was Tag's voice, full of concern. Justice wanted to tell him not to worry, but nothing seemed to be working right. Maybe that was Ian's grand plan—drug him and then sell him to . . . space pirates. Or whoever.

"Why's he mumbling about space pirates?" he heard Tag ask.

"Grab me a bag of saline," Ian answered. "Don't want him dehydrating."

Justice finally managed to open his eyes.

"Hey, Justice—you're okay. Your leg's stitched up and you've got a concussion. But you'll be fine."

"What about you?" His voice was so low that Ian had to move close to hear it. He was practically whispering in Ian's ear.

"What about me?" Ian asked.

"You have no loyalty," Justice murmured.

"Yeah, I do," Ian told him. "'S'why I'm here."

"Promise?" Justice held up his scarred hand.

Ian glanced at it. "Taggart has that scar too."

"I know. I gave it to him."

Ian wasted no time in holding Justice's hand, giving it a light squeeze. "Promise."

Tag stepped into the bedroom and tossed Ian the bag of IV fluid. Ian caught it one-handed, glanced down at it, and shook his head. "This is glucose solution. And it's expired."

Tag shrugged. "Like I know the difference. The saline solution is probably expired, too." The guy who'd built this prepper box of a cabin had stocked the basement with enough food and medical supplies to run a hospital for months. Sure, Tag had picked up some meds and bandages before coming back here, but while Tag had basic first aid knowledge, thanks to his mom's insistence on learning survival skills, he wasn't up on the more advanced crap.

Ian shook his head. "Saline doesn't degrade the way glucose does. We can probably still use it."

"The IV supplies are in the basement," Tag said. "Help yourself."

He and Ian had faked some great cheeriness when Justice was awake, but now they were back to strained silence and dark looks, which was exactly what he got as Ian brushed past him on his way to the basement.

"Trouble in paradise?" Justice asked, watching him with drowsy eyes as he dragged the corner chair over to the bed and sat down.

"Didn't know you considered Alaska paradise."

Justice shuddered. "Fucking snow. Cold. Reminds me of Christmas."

Taken aback by the anger in Justice's voice, Tag frowned. "You love Christmas." Even as he said it, he regretted it, realizing the stupidity of his statement.

Through the glaze that dulled Justice's eyes, more anger sparked. "Itor."

Yeah, Itor. The fuckers had killed their mothers on Christmas day. They'd been at Justice's mom's place for the holiday, and while their moms cooked Christmas dinner, Tag and Justice had gone to a movie. What they'd returned . . .

Tag shook his head to clear it, not willing to let himself fall down that pit of despair right now. There was plenty of time for that later.

Justice reached up, touched his head, and winced. "What did your lover drug me with?"

Tag chose to not take Justice's bait. "No idea. You got all combative and shit, and he had to sedate you."

"You let him?" Justice glared. At least, he attempted to. The drug was kicking his ass. "He could've killed me."

Tag shook his head. "He's not a bad guy, Justice."

"He lied to you," he slurred. "Got you kidnapped."

Tag wasn't sure when he would stop feeling like he'd been gut punched every time his kidnapping came up. "I know," he said. "And I'm still not over that. But haven't you done things at ACRO, *for* ACRO, that you aren't proud of?"

"I've never deceived anyone like that." Justice's voice was a curious combination of angry and high as a kite. "Never hurt an inn . . . cent."

Innocent. Ah, the drug-induced-speech-impediment stage was fun.

"Great. Glad your conscience is clear. Must be nice."

"Fuck you, Tag." Justice sighed. "You never und . . . er . . . stood why I needed to join ACRO."

Tag thought about what Ian had said, about having the security of an agency to back you up, and he had to admit that while he'd had a good run as a bartender in Florida, he'd never felt like he belonged among people he couldn't be himself with. People he had nothing in common with.

"No," Tag said quietly. "I get it. But I can't get excited about an agency like Itor."

"ACRO's nothing like Itor."

And here we go again. Did Justice never tire of sounding like a broken record? "Justice—"

Justice's hand snapped out with surprising speed to grab Tag's. He was clearly fighting the drug, but then, he'd done the same thing at the age of fourteen when he'd broken his leg. The doctors had to give him enough painkillers to knock out a horse because Justice had refused to give up control. It was why he rarely drank in college, where Tag had been Mr. Party Animal. He could still kick ass at quarters.

"I know you were shepticle . . . skephical . . ."

"Skeptical?"

Justice frowned. "Yeah. That. You were . . . skeptical. But I've been with ACRO for four years. They've been good to me. They're not in the game for power the way Itor is. They want to rid the world of scumbags." He nodded drunkenly. "Scumbags are bad."

"So, what, ACRO is a big band of superheroes who save kittens, wear white capes, and shit rainbows?"

"Don't be a dumbass." He patted Tag's hand like he was a child. "They counter the bad guys. And maybe save kittens. I'm not saying everyone at ACRO is a decent person, or that they're even nice. Trust me, ACRO is full of shitheads." He jammed his finger into his chest, except his coordination was off, and he nailed his nipple. "Am one of them. But . . . dare you to find a job where that isn't the case."

Justice had a point. Tag had worked with some dicks, some criminals even, on the crab boat and at the bar. Hell, he was pretty sure he put himself on Itor's radar when he ended up in a police report for stopping a bar employee from assaulting a woman in an alley. The employee's claim that Tag had "used his mind to smash a dumpster into him" had been met with a lot of rolled eyes, but his statement had, nevertheless, been recorded.

So, yep, Tag had worked with jerks everywhere.

But he still wasn't ready to start waving ACRO flags and marching in parades.

Justice squeezed his hand. "I'm sorry Itor got you. If I'd known, I'd have found a way to help you. I wouldn't have let you suffer."

Ooh, now it was time for intoxicated lies and oaths no one kept when they were sober.

He shrugged like it was no big deal, but inside, the wounds Itor had inflicted still bled. "I got away. Thanks to ACRO," he added grudgingly.

"How did you escape?"

By the skin of his teeth, that was how. "I was at the Madrid office when ACRO attacked. Nearly got killed." Shifting, he turned and peeled up his shirt to reveal his lower back and the messy scar there. "There was a massive explosion. Got smashed by a burning beam. And I have a nice bullet hole in my thigh. Wouldn't have survived if I hadn't made it to one of Itor's clients, a quack who runs an illegal plastic surgery facility on Madrid's outskirts."

"Madrid?" Justice croaked.

Tag nodded, decided not to go into more detail. Justice was starting to look "shocky" again, as Ian had put it, going pale and starting to sweat, and now probably wasn't the time to tell him that Tag had been forced to kill an ACRO agent during the battle.

"Hey." Tag tugged a blanket up over Justice's shoulders. "Maybe you should rest—"

"I'm sorry, Tag," Justice whispered. "I'm so sorry about Madrid. I didn't know."

"It's okay. You couldn't have known Itor'd grabbed me."

For some reason, Justice shook his head. "Madrid . . . you could have died."

"It's okay," he repeated. "Don't blame yourself. Fuck, Justice, if anyone needs to apologize, it's me. I should have gone to ACRO with you. You were right. If I'd done it, our moms would have been safe. They're dead because of me—"

Suddenly, Justice jacked into a sit and had one hand fisted in Tag's shirt. Justice's eyes were glassy, but his expression was as intense and angry as Tag'd ever seen it.

"I was wrong," he growled. "I shouldn't have said that."

"But you believe it."

"I did, once. I was angry for a long time. But now . . . I know you weren't ready for ACRO. It wouldn't have been a good fit, and we'd have been driven apart anyway." He closed his eyes, and when he opened them, those gorgeous blues were cast in shadow. "I said what I said because I was trying to punish you for choosing a normal life over me and ACRO. And I think I was trying to punish you for . . . for loving Ian."

Taggart had more apologizing to do, but Justice was flagging, his eyes going unfocused again as he fell back down on the mattress.

"Ian's here to help me."

"He could be lying."

"He's not. He told me about something called a P-128S chip that Itor planted inside his shoulder to track him. He didn't have to tell me about it. He didn't have to ask me to destroy it. But he did, and now Itor's going to know he's not playing their game. They'll kill him for that, Justice. He put his life on the line for me."

"P-128S chip . . ." Justice scowled. "Sounds familiar. You destroyed it?"

"It was his idea."

Justice snorted softly. "So everything's all great in Taggart-loves-Ian land?"

"Not by a long shot. He lied and fucked me over hard. But I believe he regrets it, and I believe he came here to help."

"You didn't deny that you love him."

Because that would be a lie. Tag looked down at his feet. Swallowed. Inhaled. Swallowed again. "I love you, Justice. Always have. I didn't think I'd love anyone again after you, but somehow I fell for him. I don't expect you to like him, but will you at least try to not be a dick to him? He's here to help. Give him a chance."

Justice yawned, and his eyes drifted closed. "You gonna tell him the same thing?"

"Yes." For all the good it would do. He didn't know if these two would ever get along.

"Fuck." Justice's eyes remained closed, and his fists, once clenched, relaxed as the meds finally won out over his will. "Don't wanna lose you again. Can't lose you again."

Oh, and here was the worst stage of intoxication: the heartfelt confessions and declarations of love you regretted when you woke up the next day.

Which made what Tag said next even worse, because he didn't have the excuse of being drunk or drugged.

"Justice," he whispered. "I don't want to lose you either."

Thankfully, he doubted Justice heard.

By the time Ian had dug through all the prepper's boxes of medical supplies and came back up from the basement with the saline bag, Justice had drifted off to sleep again.

Must be nice. Not that Ian begrudged an injured guy sleep, but damn, Ian felt like he could snooze for a week. He hadn't realized how exhausted he was until just now, when it seemed as if every muscle was protesting the climb up the stairs from the basement. Even his head was starting to hurt.

He shook it off and sank onto the mattress next to Justice and prepped the back of the guy's hand for the IV.

"You look like shit," Tag said, and yeah, that was helpful.

"It's been a long day."

"You sure what I did to the chip isn't affecting you?"

Strangely, the area surrounding the chip felt fine. There was only a little residual soreness, and Ian figured that would be gone by morning. "I'm sure. How was Justice while I was downstairs?"

As he threaded the line into Justice's vein, Tag reported, "He woke up and talked to me for a while, but he seemed pretty out of it."

"Yeah, he's a little shocky. That's to be expected. This should help. As long as he woke up and was semilucid, he's okay to sleep another hour. We'll keep waking him through the night."

"Fine by me." Tag moved to lean against the wall and watched him finish setting up the IV.

Ian turned Justice's hand over, and his fingers fell open, revealing the long, thin mark on his palm. The one that was identical to Tag's.

A sour feeling swirled in Ian's belly. Tag and Justice had so much history between them, so many stories Ian couldn't touch. He'd never been one to give in to jealousy, but this time, he couldn't help it. The marks on Justice and Taggart's palms were physical evidence that their relationship went beyond simple memories.

"You never told me about the scar," he blurted, knowing how petty it sounded but not caring.

Tag shrugged. "Never asked."

God, Tag hadn't changed a bit. Ian didn't know whether to be angry or grateful. "And I guess we don't have to now, right?"

"Really? You want to pretend we had a relationship where we talked about things?"

"We fucking did, Taggart. Don't shit on that memory."

"I'm not the one who did that first."

"Fine. Whatever." Ian pushed off the mattress and headed toward the door.

Taggart called after him, "Ian . . . we were kids."

Ian paused, hand on the doorjamb. "Pretty serious scar for kids."

"Well, now that you know Justice, you see that he's a pretty serious guy."

"He can be intense, yes. But so can you."

"I'm going to take that as a compliment."

Ian didn't answer him one way or the other, mainly because he knew it would annoy Taggart . . . but also because he knew he couldn't stay and listen to anything more about Tag and Justice's love for each other.

CHAPTER 10

J ustice was beautiful when he was sleeping.

Tag watched him from the corner chair in the bedroom, a bottle of bourbon nearly touching the floor as it dangled from his fingers. For the first time since Justice arrived at the cabin, he looked like he had before that day four years ago when Itor had destroyed their lives. Gone was the steely-eyed, guarded agent who could so easily have shot Ian and tossed him out for the wolves, just as he'd said. Now, in deep slumber, Justice looked peaceful. Relaxed. And even with the bandages, he looked sexy as hell.

Taggart could still remember the first time he'd thought of Justice in that way. At least, the first time he'd admitted to himself that he was attracted to the other boy.

They'd been seventeen, and Justice was sleeping over because his mom was helping out a friend, and they'd needed his room for a few nights. Tag and Justice had slept in the same room often enough, and it wasn't a big deal for the two of them to share a bed when they had to.

Fine. Great. No problem. But although Justice had known he was gay for most of his life, Taggart had been a little slow on the uptake. He'd been athletic, a total jock who attracted the cheerleaders, and he'd been happy to take what they offered.

Then that morning . . . Jesus, he could still see it in his mind, as clear as it'd been all those years ago.

The sun had been on the horizon, its hazy rays peeking through the dusty slats of his bedroom blinds. The mattress had been jiggling in a slow, rhythmic bounce and his first, sleep-fogged thought had been that they were experiencing a mild earthquake.

We're not even in frigging California.

Taggart managed to peel his eyes open to see if Justice was awake and feeling the same thing. And yeah, the other boy was awake. His head was kicked back into the pillow, his face contorted in what Tag first thought was agony.

Instantly alert, Tag swept his gaze lower, sure the guy was suffering from some horrible illness. But holy shit . . . he got real clear on what was happening a heartbeat later.

One of Justice's big hands rested on his bare stomach, and the other was beneath the blankets, moving up and down. The impressive tent at his groin grew larger as he worked his cock, and Taggart's mouth went so dry he thought he might choke.

He knew he shouldn't watch. Knew he should close his eyes and go back to sleep. But watching Justice jerk off was somehow the biggest turn-on of his teenaged life. And he'd seen his share of girly magazines and pornos. Not to mention that just last weekend, Heidi Cummings had given him his first blowjob in the back of her daddy's Chevy, and watching her blonde head bob on his dick had set him off embarrassingly fast.

Now, watching Justice was threatening to make him come all over himself with no physical stimulation at all.

A fine sheen of sweat glistened on Justice's chest as his muscles clenched and his body strained under the onslaught of pleasure. What would he do if Tag reached over and . . . and what? Helped? His buddy had everything under control. Besides, Taggart had never been with a guy, and when and if he decided to test those waters, he wouldn't choose Justice as his first. He couldn't risk their friendship. He might not have a lot of life experience, but he'd learned enough from his mother to know that truly good friends were the family you chose for yourself, and they were few and far between.

But that didn't stop him from having to bite his tongue to suppress a groan as Justice's body arched and his strokes came faster. His lips parted as he began to pant, and damn, Taggart wanted to taste that mouth, to dive inside it and kiss the shit out of his friend as Justice came.

Justice shoved his free hand under the covers and lifted them as his climax took him, and Tag's mouth watered—honest-to-God watered— as cum shot from the tip of his cock to his sweat-drenched abs and chest.

Taggart's own cock was rock hard and throbbing, his balls tight with the need to blow. Somehow, he remained silent and still, keeping his breathing controlled and steady, until Justice swung off the bed, his underwear and sleep pants tugged down in front, and dashed off to the bathroom.

With a sigh of relief, Tag palmed his cock, and in five strokes, he was there. The orgasm hit him so hard he saw stars. Quickly, he grabbed a sock off the floor, cleaned himself up, and was eyes closed and faking sleep before Justice even shut off the water.

That image had become Taggart's masturbation fantasy of choice for years, even long after he and Justice parted ways. Hell, he'd gone to that place in his head as recently as last year, after Ian had destroyed him.

So yeah, Justice had always been there, taking up real estate where he didn't belong. And that pissed off Tag more than anything else.

The guy had always been in his head and heart. And now he was in his bed, too. How was he supposed to deal with that?

"He'll be okay, you know."

Tag looked up to see Ian standing in the doorway, one shoulder braced against the frame, his stockinged feet crossed at the ankles. They hadn't spoken since the strained conversation earlier. He'd wanted to give Ian some space, sure, but frankly, Tag hadn't *wanted* to talk. Not when his brain was still processing everything that'd happened in the last twenty-four hours.

"Yeah, I know he'll be okay," Tag said. "Justice has always been a tough bastard."

"Then why the bedside vigil?"

Tag eyed Ian as he took a swig from the bottle. God, the guy was good-looking. "It's what we do. I got pneumonia when I was eleven, and he was there, day and night. When he broke his leg when he was fourteen, I didn't leave his side until he could walk on his own."

He'd even bypassed nurses, doctors, and security in those first few hours after Justice had arrived at the hospital, because fuck if anyone was keeping him away from his friend. Not family, they'd said? Screw that. Family had nothing to do with blood.

He glanced away from Ian before he did something stupid, like take his hand and pull him down on top of him. Not for sex, but for comfort.

"I hate that you have that kind of history with him."

Tag blinked. "What?"

"It's that jealousy thing again. You've got twenty-six years of history with him, and I can't compete with that."

He watched the steady rise and fall of Justice's chest. How many times had he laid his head on that chest and just listened to his strong heartbeat? "It doesn't have to be a competition."

"Doesn't it?" Ian murmured. "You have to choose one of us. Or have you already made that decision?"

Panic tightened his rib cage, squeezing his heart so hard he felt actual pain. He couldn't make a decision. Not again. He'd been cornered into a choice before—Justice and ACRO or nothing at all, and he'd chosen poorly. Clearly, his judgment was suspect.

"I don't know what to do, Ian. I'd rather ride out on my snow machine and meet Itor by myself than lose one of you." He gave a bitter snort. "You're right. I do run when things get real."

"And this is as real as it gets." Ian scrubbed his hand over his face, and it didn't escape Tag's notice that his fingers were trembling. "I don't want to lose you, Tag. I'll do anything. I'll share you with him if I have to. I can learn to like him. He *is* kinda hot."

Tag had a feeling that last bit was thrown in to test *his* jealousy factor . . . and oddly enough, he didn't feel jealous at all. These were the two loves of his life in this room, and if anything, this felt right.

Which was so wrong.

He shoved to his feet. "I can't talk about this right now." He started to push past Ian, but the guy grabbed him, spun him, and put his back to the wall.

"We don't have to talk," Ian growled. "But I have to do this."

He slanted his mouth over Tag's. Somehow, Ian always knew what Tag wanted, and right now, he wanted comfort. Human contact. Reassurance that he wasn't alone in being confused but still in love.

And so did Ian.

Tag's tongue slipped between Ian's lips, and that fast, the temperature in the room shot up ten degrees. Ian's hands gripped his shoulders so hard that sweet pain shot through both Tag's arms.

"You know what made me fall for you?" Ian whispered against Tag's mouth. "Life."

"What?"

Ian spoke as he kissed his way along Tag's jaw. "I didn't feel alive until I met you. And you . . . you are life. I've never met anyone who just wanted to be normal. To have a life where you take the day off to rent jet skis or go to a concert in the park at dusk."

Tag smiled, the memories of their days at the beach and concerts seeming so distant, given the cold, the snow, and the fact that Christmas was just days away. "That's why I fell for *you*, Ian . . . Oh, yeah, right there . . ."

Ian's hands had dropped to his ass, his mouth to his throat, and his erection was cozying up to Tag's. "I felt safe with you. Needed. Things I hadn't felt since Justice. You were full of life. You still can be—"

Ian cut him off with a brutal kiss, as if it was the last one they'd ever share. It wasn't. It couldn't be.

"I need you," he murmured against Ian's lips.

Ian's hands found his fly, ripped it open, and then Tag's cock was in Ian's fist. "I'm so going to fuck you."

No. He wasn't ready for that. And weirdly, the fact that he hadn't fucked Justice yesterday played a role in his hesitation. He couldn't give himself to one man but not the other. Besides—

With a growl, he yanked Ian out of the bedroom and into the living room. "You fucked me when you betrayed me to Itor," he said. He didn't mean to be cruel; if anything, he needed closure on that. "My turn."

He spun Ian around and slammed him forward over the back of the couch. Roughly, he jerked Ian's jeans and long johns down, leaving them tangled around his feet so he couldn't move. As he straightened, he smoothed his hands up Ian's long, muscular legs until he reached that sweet ass.

Spreading his cheeks with his thumbs, Tag pressed the flat of his tongue against Ian's balls and licked upward, over his puckered hole and through the deep valley, all the way to the small of Ian's back. Ian mumbled something, but Tag didn't catch it, didn't care. All that mattered was burying himself balls-deep inside the only man besides Justice he'd ever loved.

He gave himself a couple of strokes, and then cursed. "Hold on. Condom."

Ian's hand came around and gripped Tag's hip before he could move. "Don't need one. Pac-1 injection."

Tag's sex-logged brain didn't process that for a second, but, right . . . at Itor, he'd also been injected with the combined contraceptive/anti-STD drug all of the super-agent types used.

It was the one thing Tag could thank Itor for, he supposed.

But there was still the matter of lube . . .

Three feet away, on the counter, was a crock of butter. *That'll do.*

Keeping one hand on Ian's back, Tag stretched for the crock, knocked the lid off, and dipped a finger inside.

"Hurry, Tag," Ian said, his tone just shy of begging.

It took Tag two seconds to coat his erection and guide it to Ian's waiting entrance. He wasn't going to last once he was inside Ian, so he took the entry slow and easy for as long as he could stand it.

He watched the head disappear, Ian's tight ass drawing him in. "Damn," he breathed. "I forgot how . . . good you feel."

Ian moaned and pushed back in response, taking Taggart deep. Silky heat surrounded him as Ian clenched and rotated his hips, demanding more. Hell, yes, after a year of missing this firm ass, he was going to get more.

He pulled back, nearly withdrawing, before punching his hips forward in a single, powerful thrust. Ian shouted in pleasure, just as Tag knew he would. Ian had always liked taking it a little rough, and Tag liked giving it to him.

He thrust again, harder, and the sofa scored the floor as it moved with Ian. Again, harder, and Ian had to brace his arms on the cushions as his hips banged into the back of the couch. Again, but this time, Tag reached around and fisted Ian's cock.

Butter still coated his fingers, and he used it to lube that thick erection as he stroked. He circled his thumb over the crown, making Ian hiss and his cock jerk in Tag's palm. He moved his hand lower, to Ian's tight sac, skimming the pads of his fingers over the sensitive skin before pressing up into the seam and rolling one firm testicle in the way that drove Ian crazy.

Sure enough, Ian began a frenzied pumping rhythm that Tag couldn't take, not when he was already on the verge of orgasm. Bending over Ian's back, he kissed his spine as they ground against each other, taking and giving, the hard column in Tag's hand pulsing in his grip.

Outside, the wind howled, fueling the storm of ecstasy raging through Tag as he pounded against Ian. Ian was urging him to fuck harder, and the slap of flesh on flesh joined the blizzard's fury outside.

"Ian," he rasped. "Jesus—"

A lightning strike of pleasure streaked through him, making him dizzy as the climax took him. He roared in blissful release, and Ian, usually the loud one, groaned as his hot cum splashed on Tag's hand. The room spun, and so did Tag's mind, because this had been the best sex he and Ian ever had. Yes, they'd had more creative sex, more foreplay, more positions. They'd definitely fucked harder and longer.

But this had been vital in a way none of the other times had been. Ian and Tag been through hell and back, and here they were, older, wiser, and more honest than before.

The orgasm had been great.

The connection was better.

Fuck, he was a sap, wasn't he?

Wrapping his arms around Ian, he guided them both to the floor, snagging the blanket draped over the couch on the way down. He twisted so they were sitting with their backs to the sofa, Ian leaning against Tag's chest. He dragged the blanket across their laps and relaxed in the flickering light from the fire.

It felt good and right, and the weirdest thing was that he wished Justice would come out of the bedroom. Right now.

If he did, Tag would get up and kiss him. Just push him up against the wall and kiss him with the mouth that had just kissed Ian. What would Justice do if he did that? What would Ian do?

His cock stirred at the thought, the horny bastard.

The wind had died down, and the silence, broken only by the sound of their heavy breathing and the fire crackling in the corner, must have been too quiet, because he opened his mouth ... and stupid shit fell out.

"Did you mean it when you said you'd share me?"

Ian moaned a muffled, "Mm ... hmm."

Don't say it! Don't say— "What if I shared ... you? And Justice."

Ian's drowsy eyes shot open. "You saying what I think you're saying?"

Yeah, Tag couldn't believe he was saying it, either. But he couldn't lose either one of them. And really, he truly thought that if Ian and Justice could get past their distrust, they'd find they had a lot in common. They were both homebodies, preferring to stay in rather than party at a bar. They both read geeky books. And they both had an unholy love of raw oysters.

Shudder.

"I know it sounds crazy," Tag said, "but I think you guys could hit it off." *Right, because a shared love of science fiction novels and oysters on the half shell was all you needed for a happily ever after.*

"I don't know, Tag . . ."

"It's not conventional," he said quickly. "But neither are our lives. Justice said I'm selfish, and in this, he's right. I want you both."

"Justice will never go for it."

Well, that wasn't a no. "He just needs some patience and time. It can't hurt to try." He grinned. "And I know just how to test the waters."

CHAPTER 11

The next twenty-four hours went by quickly for Ian. He and Tag had settled into a comfortable rhythm, taking turns staying with Justice, talking, sharing meals. He didn't make any moves on Tag; Tag knew how he felt, and the ball was in his court.

But man, it killed him to not pounce on Tag, take him to the floor, and pound into that big body until they both passed out. They could rest against the couch the way they had last night. When they'd been touching. Kissing. Enjoying the silence.

Until Tag had sprung the craziest idea ever on him. And it *was* crazy, right?

Ian had no one to blame but himself though; he'd told Tag he'd share him if he had to. But he'd have to share more than just Tag, wouldn't he? He'd have to share himself.

He'd barely been able to give himself to Tag, so how was he going to share any part of himself with Justice? Was there enough of him to go around?

A million questions bounced inside his head as he put down the dusty copy of *The Call of the Wild* he'd found in a drawer. He hadn't been reading so much as staring blankly at the pages anyway.

Because Justice freaking snored.

He looked over at the man sleeping like a log, sprawled out on the queen-sized bed like he owned it. He'd kicked the covers off, leaving his long, lean body bare except for maroon boxer briefs. Which had a *very* nice bulge in them.

Stop staring. He's injured, for Christ's sake.

Not that Ian was feeling one hundred percent himself—he was somewhere in the sixty percent range but doing a damned good job of faking it. In an attempt to be noble, he slid his gaze to Justice's damaged leg. The stitches looked great. Kudos to Tag for keeping a kickass medical stash. In anticipation of a battle or prolonged siege, the guy had, on his way to the cabin, stocked up on meds, so his supply was pretty damned decent. Ian wasn't going to ask how or where he'd scored the stuff, though. It was enough to know that Justice was on antibiotics to stave off infection, and when he'd been in pain, the drugs were available.

Fortunately, painkillers were no longer needed.

Physically, Justice was sleeping less and rousing more easily. His pupils were equal and reactive.

He was on the mend, and not a moment too soon. Because Itor had to be getting close, despite the storm. The only good thing was that Ian had several days lead time on them, and he knew that Justice had a plane that could at least get Tag to safety.

But Justice would have to be up to flying the damn thing first, and Ian wasn't sure if that timing would match Itor's arrival—which was a when, not if, situation.

Danger was always a relentless master. Itor was synonymous with that.

The savory aroma of stew drifted into the bedroom from the kitchen, where Tag was whipping them up some dinner. He'd always been a good cook. Ian hoped that translated to being good with moose or elk or God-only-knew-what meat he'd dumped into the stew earlier.

Suddenly, Justice began to shift in his sleep. His face looked pained and he was mumbling something. Holding out his hands like he was telling someone or something to stop.

Then, "Shit...no...he's inside. I didn't know. You have to believe me...I didn't fucking know."

And then he began to try to get up and out of bed, which wasn't the best idea on that ankle of his. It wasn't broken, but it was a bad sprain that wouldn't allow him to put weight on it at the moment. The stitches added to his vulnerability and would split easily if his ankle turned again.

Ian shot up from the corner chair and put firm hands on Justice's shoulders, pinning him to the mattress. Of course, it didn't stop the guy from struggling, but when Ian put his full strength behind it, no one except another Excedo was getting past his grip. "Justice, babe, wake up—you're having a dream."

Finally, Justice was still, although he continued to mumble a little. And then he opened his eyes, grabbed the front of Ian's shirt, fisting it, pulling him in close.

"I was there, Ian," Justice whispered, his voice urgent and raw.

"Justice, you're dreaming."

"Not anymore. No. Listen . . . I was with ACRO when they bombed Itor. The Madrid office where Tag was."

Ah, fuck. "You didn't know."

"No. But still. Jesus, I was responsible for almost killing him." Justice let go of his shirt and lay back down fully on the pillow.

"It was my fault he was there."

"And his, for being too pigheaded to follow me. Then again . . ."

"What?"

Justice shrugged. "He'd never have met you."

Ian blinked, then managed, "I figured you would've liked it that way."

"Maybe I thought that when I first met you. But now . . ."

But now . . .

Did he really just thank Ian for being in Tag's life? What the fuck kind of meds were they giving him? "And did you call me babe before?" he demanded.

Ian blew out a breath, shook his head. "You're a piece of work, Justice, you know that?"

"Is that some kind of backhanded compliment?"

"Yes," Ian said firmly.

He glanced up at Ian. Right before his nightmare about Madrid, he'd been dreaming about something else. Or, at least he thought he'd been dreaming. But Ian's shirt was ripped in front, in the same place Tag had ripped it in Justice's dream. When Tag and Ian were kissing. And then . . . fucking.

Which meant . . . yeah, that had happened. Nice. Like interactive porn. With the love of his life and an Excedo-Seducer-traitor he was supposed to hate and couldn't stop looking at. All while he was trying to recover from being hit by a tree.

But there'd also been talking. Justice strained his memory, trying to recall what he'd heard. There were words like *merc* and *love* and *share*.

"What if I shared you?"

It didn't matter if it was hazy and Justice couldn't process it completely. Because it all pointed to one thing—Tag had forgiven Ian. And Tag obviously loved him. Fuck. But it's not like Ian hadn't made sacrifices for Tag.

"I know," Justice slurred a little. "Tag told me you had him deactivate your P-128S chip. Big risk."

"Worth it," Ian said.

Justice snorted. "Were you aware of all the consequences of disarming it?"

"I'm aware that I could've died while Tag tampered with it."

"Did you tell him that?" Justice asked.

"Are you kidding? He wouldn't have done it."

Justice felt a grudging thread of respect for Ian for realizing that. "What else?"

"I knew that disarming it would put me on Itor's hit list." Ian rolled his eyes. "I'm not an idiot, Justice, and grilling me is only going to make you see that sooner than later."

Doubtful. "Are you worried?"

"Not about that, but I am worried about you."

Justice wasn't sure he'd heard Ian correctly. "Me? You're worried about *me*?"

Ian gave him a lopsided smile. "Believe it or not, yes. But you'll be fine. Tag on the other hand?" He sighed deeply, looked over his shoulder, then asked in a low voice, "Will ACRO take him? Really?"

"Yeah, really. Why?" Justice couldn't help but challenge. "Reconsidering your strategy?"

"Maybe."

Justice tilted his head. "Is this some kind of reverse psychology?"

"No, this is trying to do right by Tag."

"And if I wasn't here? What would you be doing? Bringing Tag to me at ACRO . . . or taking him on the run, fucking him the whole time?" Justice could hear the hurt in his own voice.

"I do love fucking him, Justice." Ian's voice held a quiet memory that made Justice want to shake it out of him, spill it on the floor, break it so neither Ian nor Taggart remembered it.

But it was no use. There was a bond between them, as obvious as the sun in the sky, and there was no reason to fight that. Devlin had taught him that one of the most important things in life was knowing when to fight and when to walk away.

"He's not okay, you know," Justice said now.

"I know. But he will be," Ian assured him. "He's getting there."

"Bet you make it better for him."

"I tried, Justice. I really tried."

Justice swallowed hard. "And you want to keep trying."

"I can't lie about that."

"Didn't ask you to." Justice's arm throbbed, but so did his dick. Jesus, what the hell was in this medication? He picked the bottle up, and it slid from his fingers. He cursed, leaned over the side of the bed, and almost rolled off.

At the last second, strong arms grabbed him and gently rolled him back. He looked right into Ian's eyes and saw more concern there than he ever thought possible.

Before he could stop himself, he cupped the back of the man's neck and pulled him close, kissed him hard and fast. Moaned "Ian" into his mouth when Ian took over the kiss, grabbing Justice's hair to deepen the kiss.

God, Ian was a good kisser. Didn't matter what hurt on Justice—this kiss was enough to make him forget everything.

Almost everything.

"Don't stop on my account." Tag's voice was rough and came from somewhere over Ian's shoulder. "I'll be happy to direct though."

Justice wondered for a brief second if Tag was pissed, but hell, he didn't sound it at all. He sounded . . . turned on.

As turned on as Justice felt. As if to prove it to both of them, Tag moved closer, just as Ian rubbed his pelvis against Justice's, the friction enough to make Justice groan into Ian's mouth. Justice covered Tag's jean-clad cock with his palm, and Tag grabbed his wrist and pressed his hand hard against the bulge.

And then Ian broke the kiss, sucked hard on the side of Justice's neck. Nipped at the sensitive skin, even as Tag murmured, "We'll take care of you, all right?"

Jesus. This was better than porn. Better than anything because Tag was here with him. Touching him. And, for the moment, not angry at him.

But fuck, his cock needed way more attention.

He pushed his hand inside his briefs, began to stroke himself. Ian stopped kissing him, and he opened his eyes to see that both he and Taggart were just watching him get off, both of their breaths quickening at the lewd movements happening under the cloth.

Taggart reached down and pulled the underwear over his hand and cock. He let out a stuttered breath as Ian leaned in to swipe a drop of pre-cum, then spread it around his crown.

"You're recovering," Tag told him with mock seriousness. "Shouldn't have to do the work yourself."

"He sure looks good doing it, though," Ian said, right before he sucked on one of Justice's nipples, taking it between his teeth. He almost jumped through the ceiling, but Tag knew him so damned well—still—and was already holding him steady to ensure that wouldn't happen.

He could barely move, between the accident and the two bodies hovering over his . . . and for once, he didn't give a damn.

Tag put a hand on his wrist, gently tugged Justice's hand away. It was quickly replaced by Ian's hand, wrapping around Justice's cock, and again, thinking ceased. Because who the hell cared about the why—he was way more interested in the *are these two going to make me come right now* scenario.

The imminent answer seemed to be a yes.

CHAPTER 12

Tag had never seen anything hotter in his life than one man he loved stroking the other man he loved. After all the shit that'd gone down over the years—hell, in the last few hours—they all needed this.

Sure, Justice needed to heal physically, but they all had a lot of emotional healing to do.

Perspiration beaded on Justice's forehead as he arched into Ian's hand, his thighs and abs straining, his chest heaving.

"Faster," Taggart said as he sank onto the mattress and brushed his lips across Justice's. "Make him come."

Ian must have obeyed because suddenly Justice was crying out in erotic agony, alternating curses with "Yes" and "Holy . . . yeah."

Justice's arm came around Tag, dragging him down to lie next to him as he recovered, while Ian went to the bathroom and returned with a wet washcloth. Tag watched as Ian cleaned up Justice gently, the same way he'd performed all the medical tasks. Tag had been on the receiving end of Ian's care several times, so he didn't know why he was so shocked by the tenderness now, but he was. And his heart swelled.

Still, he was afraid to hope for anything beyond this moment. Not when they still had Itor—and ACRO—to deal with.

Justice was sound asleep by the time Ian finished. Tag dragged the blanket up to Justice's chin and joined Ian in the living room.

Wordlessly, Ian took Tag in his arms and just held him.

"Hey," Tag said. "You okay?"

"Yeah." Ian cleared his throat. "Just . . . thank you. I've never had that before."

Tag pulled back a little so he could look into Ian's eyes. "You're a Seducer. You're saying you've never had a threesome?"

Hurt flashed in Ian's eyes, and he went taut. "I have, but I wasn't talking about that." He jerked away from Tag, and shit, Tag had really put his foot in his mouth, hadn't he?

"I'm sorry—"

"'S'okay. You couldn't know what I meant."

"What *did* you mean?"

Shaking his head, Ian shoved his feet into his boots. "I'm going to do a quick patrol of the area."

"Dammit, Ian, don't shut down on me." Tag reached out, but Ian dodged him, and he let his arm fall uselessly to his side. "Please, Ian. Tell me what you meant."

Ian strapped on his snowshoes and grabbed his parka. "I meant . . . Fuck me, I meant that I've never had . . . *that*. People around me who care. Like it's not just sex." He didn't face Tag. "Thank you."

He escaped the cabin like his feet were on fire and the snow outside was going to save his life.

Shit. Granted, the threesome thing was Tag's first, but he'd grown up surrounded by people who cared. The last four years had been hell, not having that anymore . . . not until Ian. Which'd gotten FUBARed bad.

Figuring Ian needed some time alone to get his thoughts together, Tag checked and double-checked the monitors and the cabin's security backup systems, and when he was done, he settled into the kitchen to finish making dinner.

The pot of stew had simmered for long enough, and the savory scent of venison and beer gravy made his mouth water. But stew always needed biscuits. Justice's mom had taught Tag that. She used to say that it was up to Tag to keep her family recipe alive, since Justice had never gotten the hang of cooking anything that didn't come in a can or a macaroni-and-cheese box.

He'd just finished making enough biscuits to feed an army—or Itor—when Justice shambled out of the bedroom in a pair of sweats he must have pilfered from Tag's dresser. Bless his heart, he wasn't wearing a shirt, just the way Tag always liked him.

"Just checked my phone," Justice said. "Still no signal."

"Storms always knock out comms." He gestured to the couch. "Sit. You shouldn't be walking on that leg. I'll bring you some food."

Justice scrubbed a hand over his face. "First, you gonna tell me if what happened in there was real?"

"Which part? When you recited poetry while dancing practically naked on the bed, or when Ian jerked you off while I kissed you?"

Justice blinked. "Ah . . ."

"All real," Tag teased. He got flipped off for his effort.

Laughing for the first time in what felt like centuries, he scooped stew into a bowl and plopped a biscuit into it as Justice limped over to the couch and sank down in front of the fire.

"Where is Ian, anyway?" Justice asked.

Tag grabbed himself a beer and then handed Justice the bowl before taking a seat on the overstuffed chair across from Justice. "Out patrolling. He should be back at any—"

Speak of the devil. Ian, clothes crusted in snow and ice, threw open the door and barreled inside. "Fuck. Fuck a fucking duck, it's fucking freezing out there. Storm's here." His teeth chattered as he stripped out of his gear. "And what, you couldn't find a hideout in Mexico or the Bahamas? Hot shower. Now." He finally noticed that Justice was up, and Tag swore the guy went the color of a beet. "Oh, ah . . . hey."

Justice turned the same color. They matched. It was sort of cute. "Hey."

There was no time for more awkwardness because Ian was off like a shot to the bathroom, and a moment later, Tag heard water running.

Which made him think of all the times they'd showered together.

Justice ducked his head and dug into his food, not coming up for air until every last bite was gone.

"More?" Tag asked.

"Thanks, no. It was good, though. You always were a damned fine cook." Justice set the bowl on the coffee table, appearing more awake and alert than he had in days. "We need to talk."

"About what happened in the bedroom? Look, it was my idea. I told Ian to—"

Justice held up a hand. "Not that. Well, maybe about that. Later. Right now I want to talk to you about you coming back to ACRO with me."

Oh. That. Buzzkill. Tag would rather talk about Justice having an orgasm in Ian's hand.

"I can't."

"You won't."

Tag shook his head. "It's not that simple, Justice."

"From where I'm sitting, it seems pretty fucking simple to me. ACRO can protect you. Itor will either kill you or use you. Not sure how that's not the easiest choice ever."

Tag stared at the beer bottle, but it didn't look like Sam Adams had any good advice beyond *drink responsibly*. "I don't trust ACRO."

"Do you trust me?"

Just days ago, Tag would have said no, but it would have been a lie. Still, he'd have done it out of stubbornness. But the truth was that he did trust Justice. With his soul. "I trust you, but—"

"But what?" Justice asked, his voice low, soft, as if he didn't want to spook Tag. "I've been there four years, and no one has tried to experiment on me, or hurt me, or enslave me. Yes, the training is rough. The assignments can be dangerous. But you can turn them down. You can be a desk jockey if you want to. You're free, Tag. It's not a job. It's a family."

Tag's doubt must have still been obvious in his expression because Justice added, "There are people there who can manipulate the weather. Shape-shift into wolves. Talk to animals. No one feels like a freak, and when one of them gets hurt, they all rally. Give them a chance. You deserve it. *We* deserve it." Justice leaned forward, bracing his forearms on his knees. "You can always leave. Just . . . try. Please."

Tag didn't think his heart had ever beat as fast as it was right now. It was as if he were facing an angry grizzly and not the man he'd loved since he was a teen. This was a huge decision, but ultimately, there was only one way to go. He'd refused before, and now he knew that had been a mistake.

"I'll go with you," he murmured. "I'll give ACRO a chance."

Justice narrowed his eyes at Tag. "I sense a 'but' coming on."

And it was a big one. "But I hate using my powers. I don't want to be forced to use them. And I did things at Itor. I . . . I killed people."

Justice closed his eyes and blew out a long breath. When he lifted his lids, his eyes glinted with the kind of determination that had gotten them into trouble as kids. Once Justice decided something, there was no talking him out of it.

"It'll work out. ACRO isn't Itor. They won't force you to do anything you don't want to do."

"Dammit, Justice, even so, I killed . . ." He trailed off, his mouth dry, his pulse pounding in his ears. Yes, he trusted Justice, but he'd just said that ACRO was family, and this . . . this wasn't something families forgave.

"Tell me." Justice laid a hand lightly on Tag's thigh. "Who did you kill?"

"Two agents," Tag blurted, before he lost his nerve. "Two *ACRO* agents. Do you really think they're going to just let that slide?"

Justice laced his hands over his abs and leaned back on the couch, legs spread, looking completely at ease and so fucking sexy that Tag had to take a long drink of his icy beer to cool himself off. Even injured, with a bruise that extended from his hairline to his cheekbone on the right side, and his stitched leg and swollen ankle, Justice exuded a sensual masculinity that Tag had never been able to resist.

"I think they're going to take the circumstances under consideration." He pegged Taggart with a hard stare that somehow wasn't absent of sympathy. "Like I said, ACRO isn't Itor. They aren't going to force you into anything, and they aren't going to punish you."

"Maybe you're not clear on what I said. Two agents. Dead. One died because I was ordered to send his elevator plummeting thirty floors. It was an assassination, pure and simple." Not that Tag had had a choice. Itor had known exactly how to force his compliance.

"And the other?" Justice asked quietly.

"It was a couple of months ago. During ACRO's takedown of Itor."

ACRO agents had stormed Itor's Australian headquarters while simultaneously hitting all of their main satellite offices. Including the office in Spain where Tag had been working. Although "working" wasn't exactly an accurate term. More like he'd been a leashed dog, forced to do Itor's bidding. If he refused, they tortured him. If he refused again, they showed him surveillance footage of Justice and said they could get to him. Hurt him. Kill him.

Justice sat forward, bracing his forearms on his thighs. "What happened?"

Another long pull on the beer bottle. "I'd come in for a briefing. My handler wanted me to collapse a steel bridge. They didn't tell me why, but I know they were planning to steal a nuclear device. I'm betting the collapse would come after the device moved over it."

"They wanted to take out anyone in pursuit and create a massive distraction."

"That's my guess. Anyway, we came under attack. It happened so fast. No one knew who was hitting us—ACRO, the Aquarius Group, one of the rogue startup agencies—no clue. But we were getting our asses kicked."

Tag took another swig, but the alcohol wasn't helping him mute the images and sounds of people dying in horrible ways. "All I wanted was to get out of there. Leave Itor to get smashed. But the people attacking us weren't exactly handing out hall passes, you know?" Slamming the bottle down on the crate coffee table, he shoved to his feet and started to pace. "It was a bloodbath for both agencies."

And Tag had added to the bloodbath by taking out his supervisor. He'd hated the Excedo psychopath, and not even the guy's ability to lift a fucking car with his bare hands had been enough to stop a bullet to the head.

"I was trying to get out of there. Then there was an explosion, and I got pinned under a burning beam. Not sure when I took the bullet to the leg, but somehow I got out from under the beam and crawled my way to the exit. Almost made it, too, when some super-speedy son of a bitch came out of nowhere and tried to gut me with his Ka-Bar." Taggart had been wounded and bleeding, but his self-preservation instinct was strong, and he'd managed to rip the blade away with his power.

"And you took him out? He was an ACRO agent?"

Tag nodded. "I found out later. Once I got away and healed from the burn and the bullet wound, I made some calls. Everyone told me the same thing. ACRO had dismantled Itor and everyone was in the wind. I figured it was my chance to escape."

"So you came here."

Tag looked down at his stockinged feet. "I went home."

He heard Justice's sharp inhalation. "Home?"

"Yeah." He couldn't look at Justice, knew if he did he'd lose it in some incredibly nonmasculine manner, so instead he grabbed the iron poker and messed around with the fire. "We still own the second property in Montana, you know. It's in both our names."

"I know." Justice's voice sounded like it had been dragged over the gravel road that wound through the land their moms had bought for them a couple of years before they died. They'd wanted another off-the-grid location if needed, and by then, they'd assumed Tag and Justice would always be together, might even make their home there.

"I wanted to hide there, but . . ." Too many reminders. "So I came here. No address, hard to get to, and well protected. Been here about a month, and then I found out that people have been asking about me in some of the nearest villages."

"Jesus," Justice murmured. "You shouldn't have had to go through that alone."

Tag watched from out of the corner of his eye as Justice sat up straight, his muscular body tensing as if he was preparing to do battle right there on the couch. "We'll keep you safe, Tag. You'll never have to be alone again."

Tag wanted to believe him. Wanted it desperately. But if ACRO wouldn't take him, he was a dead man. Because one thing was certain; he wasn't going back to Itor. His last stand would be here, and the house he'd bought to keep himself safe would be where he died.

Fitting, he supposed, that he'd join his mom at Christmas.

"Tag?"

He shoved a log into the wood stove, because fire was so much easier to deal with than emotions. "Yeah?"

"Come here."

Tag's first instinct was to pack on his snow gear and go out to patrol. To run, just like Ian had said he did whenever shit got real. And this was as real as it got.

So Tag put on his big-boy pants and stopped playing with the fire. When he turned to Justice, the other man was patting the cushion next to him.

That was all it took. Tag was next to him in an instant. Justice's arms came around him and his mouth came down on his, and even though none of it was remotely sexual, it still felt amazing.

"You know what would make this even better?" Justice asked as he pulled back and tucked Tag's head into the curve between his shoulder and his neck.

"What?"

Justice reached up and stroked Tag's hair, lulling him into utter relaxation. He hadn't slept well in days. Weeks. Months, really. And now he felt his lids beginning to droop.

"If Ian was here with us."

If Tag hadn't already been wildly in love with Justice . . . that would have done it.

Smiling, he closed his eyes, and for the first time in forever, he slept, knowing he was safe.

CHAPTER 13

"You guys all right?" Ian asked, poking his head around the kitchen corner.

It had taken him half an hour in the shower to thaw out, and then a bowl of Tag's mystery-meat stew had warmed him even more. He actually felt almost human again. Almost, because the nagging headache was driving him nuts and his appetite was off. Apparently, Alaska didn't agree with him.

Tag motioned him closer, but he hesitated, glancing at Justice. Since they'd messed around, Justice had spent time sleeping and healing, and now, Justice was giving him a half smile, and yeah, there was something there. For all of them.

Ian had checked on them earlier and found Justice asleep, Tag resting, and hadn't wanted to disturb them. He'd known the two of them were going to talk about Tag's time at Itor when Justice woke. Obviously, they had to be alone for that, but fuck, he hated being on the outside of things.

But by the way they were watching him now . . . it was apparent that they didn't want him on the outside now. It was in their look, and then Tag made it crystal clear by motioning for him to sit at the end of the couch.

He picked up Justice's legs carefully and rested Justice's hurt ankle on his lap.

"I told Justice about the ACRO men I killed," Tag told him.

"And I told him that we'll deal with it. A lot of ACRO agents come in under not-so-perfect circumstances," Justice explained. "But it's not going to be safe here soon. We can't expect the blizzard to last forever."

In fact, they hadn't expected it to be this bad at all. They had plenty of supplies, but while the weather kept Itor out, it also locked them in . . . and Ian had never been comfortable with no escape route.

Tag had a "snow machine," as he sometimes called it, that they could take to where Ian had parked his own snowmobile before making the long haul in snowshoes to the cabin. But all three of them couldn't fit on Tag's machine. Justice could ride with Tag, and Ian could get some exercise and go on foot until they reached his snowmobile and then rode on to Justice's plane, but they couldn't do any of that during the storm. For now, they were screwed.

"Your mom would've been so proud of you," Tag said suddenly to Justice.

"I think so, yeah," Justice said quietly. "And they'd both be proud of us, Tag, for surviving."

Ian nodded. "Tag told me what happened to all of you. It sounded like they gave you both a great childhood."

One corner of Justice's mouth tipped up in a wan smile. "Our moms always pushed us to do what we wanted with our lives, as long as we were happy."

"And safe," Tag added. "I thought that's what moms did, you know?"

"Yeah, well, not all of them." Ian gave a small rueful smile, meant it to be a nothing statement, but it was too fucking loaded, and both men stared at him. "Forget it."

"I don't want to forget it," Tag said. "I told you all about how I grew up. How Justice did too."

"So what, it's my turn now?"

"Yes," Justice said emphatically.

Ian rubbed Justice's calf gently, trying to avoid both men's gazes. "I don't remember much about my mom. I was young when she died. She was killed by another merc on a job—she was a Seducer who met my dad on a job." He squeezed his eyes shut, the headache that had been behind his eyes all day suddenly getting a bit worse. *Goddamned family stress will kill you every time.* "Fuck, I don't want to do this."

"Yeah, I know," Tag sympathized.

"No, I don't think you do. Both of you, you've never had to live your lives whoring yourselves out. You've never had people look at you like that's all you're good for. After a while, trusting people becomes difficult." His words came out more harshly than he'd intended.

"Don't."

He stared at Justice. "Don't what?"

"You were going to get up. Don't."

"Now you're a mind reader?"

Tag laughed. "You'd be surprised. We all have our secret talents."

"In these few days together, I've gotten good at reading you." Justice leaned back against Tag's chest. Seeing them together, so comfortable . . .

"Ian, come on," Tag urged, "come closer."

Ian shifted so most of Justice's legs was draped over him. Tag's arm was over the back of the couch and Ian put his arm back there too, so Tag could grab his hand. Connected by Justice—both odd and fitting—Ian told them his story.

He'd been the son of a merc, a man who'd claimed he couldn't be bought by anyone. In the end, that had turned out to be the biggest lie he'd told, but he'd taught Ian two valuable lessons: trust no one, and use everyone you can.

And that's how he'd spent the last fourteen years. He'd trained as a Seducer from the time he'd been eighteen. Before that, he'd trained as a regular mercenary who could be easily hired by Itor or any of her sister agencies. Having the gift of speed as an Excedo, and more than normal strength, like his father, and his father before him, made him perfect in that role . . . but his fluid sexuality made him an even more valuable commodity. And that was recognized early on by a couple who trained Seducers. They'd come to him, offered him a yearlong internship.

"And your dad just gave you to this couple?" Justice asked.

"If it meant money? Yeah. And if it meant me getting out of my dad's house, definitely, yes." Ian heard the fierceness in his own voice. "It was a blessing and curse, you know? I had more sex than any red-blooded guy could ever want."

"And the bad?" Tag prompted.

Ian sighed. "Instead of being special, sex was just like anything else in my life—a job. A commodity. A thing that could be traded and forced, used and abused. And paid for."

That was the key. With his speed and his bedroom skills, Ian found himself in demand. When he'd been hired by Itor for some recruiting missions, he'd had the same dangerous mentality as his father—anything for the money—but he'd begun to understand how things in life could harden a man. And how he'd become so damned hardened . . . and how it didn't make any damned sense that Taggart had stripped his defenses far more easily than anyone should've been able to.

After Tag, he'd worried that he'd never be able to do his job again. And, in a way, he hadn't. Not well, at least. He'd fucked other people for Itor, but he'd been as cold as ice. And he'd never been able to stop thinking about Tag, which made him close himself off even more.

"I couldn't have stayed with Itor, couldn't have kept being a Seducer after you, Tag. There was just no way."

"I always figured a Seducer's job wasn't an easy one," Justice said, almost hesitantly. "But I never really thought about how badly it could fuck you up."

"I guess, for the Seducer who's in a committed relationship, it's different, but those are few and far between. They catch most of us when we're too young to know any better and train the idea of love right out of us. Train the idea that sex is about other people's pleasure—and how pleasure makes you stupid and vulnerable—right *into* us," Ian tried to explain. "So sex for both of you . . . it's so easy. I know things are complicated between you, but the sex? It's not what's standing in your way. For me, sex colors how I view everything. And with all the people I've been with, all the things I've seen . . . it's hard to shake that. And it's hard to view myself as anything but a Seducer, who's only value is in sex. In the job of sex."

"I'm sorry, Ian," Justice said quietly. "I know I was tough on you in the beginning about that."

"I can't blame you. I really fucked up. And I wouldn't have trusted me either," Ian assured him. "But that doesn't change how I see myself."

Tag shook his head slowly, a frown creasing his forehead. "What about how we see you? Doesn't that change anything? Because I don't see you as anything but a man, Ian. I never did."

"What about you?" Ian asked Justice.

"Want me to show you how I feel about your past? Because damn, I can put it to good use, Ian, and not think badly of you at all."

"Wait." Tag frowned. "Is that really how you see sex—that you think we see you like that?" He sounded so concerned.

"Not with you—that never happened and that's how I knew . . ." Ian shrugged, tried to look away, but Justice pressed on.

"And with me?"

"Not with you either." But fuck, this wasn't going to work. "Look, ACRO isn't going to take me. Especially not with me being on Itor's death list. I'm too much of a risk for them all around."

"So you're giving up?" Justice demanded. "Because even if you are, we're not."

Tag was smiling at Justice, then he flicked his glance to Ian. "Don't bother to argue with Mr. Black-or-White here. He really is Captain America when he gets like this."

"You can call me that in bed," Justice told them both seriously.

"Yeah, we'll take you up on that," Tag said.

"When?" Ian joked.

Justice smile was slow and lazy as he tugged his sweats down. "I've always heard you shouldn't put off tomorrow what you can do today."

CHAPTER 14

Justice's memories of Ian and Tag stroking him in the bed a couple of days ago were hazy, but fuck, they'd been good memories to keep him going as he healed. And now, seeing the appreciation clearly in Ian's eyes, having Tag literally at his back . . .

If anyone had told him last week that he'd be sharing the only man he'd loved with another guy, he'd never have believed it. Seeing Ian now . . . not so unbelievable at all.

Justice shifted on the sofa, pushing his good leg behind Ian, urging Ian closer. Ian slid so he was half on top of him, both of them in Tag's lap. And Justice carded his hand through Ian's hair and pulled him in for a kiss.

Ian had saved Tag—Justice's best friend, his first love. And Tag had fallen in love with Ian. It was only a matter of time before Justice felt Ian in his heart as well.

"Come on, you two—we'll be more comfortable in bed." Tag's voice sounded husky. Ian eased off Justice reluctantly, then bent to help him up. He wrapped an arm around Ian's shoulder and limped along to the bedroom, with Tag following.

Outside, the blizzard picked up steam—the snow and ice tinked against the metal and glass windows, the wind howled like it had a major message to send, but they were here and together and safe.

And for tonight, Justice didn't want to have to think that it could be any other way.

When they got to the bed, Justice leaned on Ian and skimmed off his sweats completely before crawling onto the mattress. Tag was stripping as he walked into the room, and Ian was shifting his gaze between them, a small smile playing on his lips.

"You two are fucking gorgeous," he growled as Tag climbed into the bed.

"You've got us in bed already, Ian," Tag teased. "Don't need to compliment us." And Justice laughed. God, it felt good to laugh.

"I'll show you compliments." Ian stripped his shirt and moved in between Justice's legs. Ian swallowed his cock, and Justice jerked and groaned and cursed while Ian hummed. Then Ian reached over and stroked Tag, as Tag tweaked Justice's nipples.

"Ian, fuck." Justice rocked his hips in time with the rhythm Ian set—it was relentless, but he wanted to come inside Ian. Although coming like this was so damned tempting.

Next time. Because there would be many more next times, dammit. Impatient, he tugged Ian's hair. Ian responded to the roughness, crawling up Justice's body.

Justice heard the click of the lube bottle, and Tag grabbed his hand and squirted lube into it, saying, "Ian likes it when you play with his ass. Start with two fingers."

Justice pulled Ian close and kissed him. In response, Ian moaned into his mouth and Justice slid his hand down and began to finger him. He pushed two lubed fingers against Ian's hole. "Yeah, ride them, Ian. Then you're going to ride me."

He maneuvered Ian onto his back, then spread the man's legs wide, working up to three fingers while Tag kissed Ian, then moved behind Justice.

For a second, Justice froze. It'd been a long time since he'd bottomed for anyone. The only one he'd ever done so for was . . .

"You okay with this?" Tag murmured.

"Only if you know it's your turn next," Justice said.

"One of you needs to fuck me now," Ian broke in.

"He's demanding. I like it." Justice leaned in and began to push inside of Ian, hard and fast, making him arch off the bed, hook a leg around Justice's hip, and use his heel to drive Justice faster.

God, Ian was beautiful too—a different kind of beautiful than Tag, who was licking and biting the shit out of his neck, no doubt leaving blossoms of red marks in a trail down to his shoulder. And he was watching. "Yeah, fuck him harder, Justice. Isn't he tight? Doesn't he feel amazing?"

"So fucking good," Justice agreed, watching Ian's eyes go glassy. "Don't come, Ian."

Tag was opening him, using his tongue first, urging Justice to glide in and out of Ian, making them both insane. And then he used lubed fingers, playing with him, fucking him with his fingers. "You ready, Justice?"

"Come on, Tag. I won't break. Fuck me, now." His voice was rough—raw, almost—and Ian groaned his approval of Justice's demands.

Finally, Tag entered him, slow at first, and then he leaned forward, putting all his weight behind it until he was balls-deep inside of Justice. Justice stilled, feeling Ian hugging his cock, with Tag throbbing inside of him. Connected.

Whole.

And then Tag began to move.

"Tag . . . Ian . . . Shit." Justice's entire body trembled as he was manipulated, driven by Tag to fuck Ian relentlessly. Ian's ankles hooked up around Tag's thighs, locking them together even further, and Justice, even more so than Ian, could do nothing but hang on for the ride.

"Go ahead," Tag told them. "Want to watch you both come." He pounded into Justice, who took Ian in the same way, until Ian came in thick, white ropes along his chest and belly. Justice's balls tightened, and Tag thrust, hitting his prostate expertly.

Everything faded into the orgasm—he was aware he was yelling both men's names, cursing, muttering incoherently, so much so that it pulled Tag into the orgasm, if the erratic jerks of his hips were any indicator.

All he could hang on to was the blissful wash of contentment that covered him in warm, rough heat.

CHAPTER 15

For the next day and a half, Justice rested while Tag and Ian patrolled the grounds, set more traps, and kept an eye on comms. They were all hoping for the reception to return and alternately dreading it, since it would mean that Itor was on their way.

If they knew where Tag was.

No functional chip in Ian, sure, but that didn't mean Itor didn't have other ways, other sources. And this cabin had been Tag's for a long time. It was only a matter of time before Itor ferreted out this intel and came for all of them.

But not if ACRO could get there first.

Late that morning, when Justice was having more coffee, he heard shouting outside—Tag—and then heard the sound of a helo racing overhead. He froze and listened.

Not one of ACROs.

"Not Itor's either," Ian confirmed, also having frozen in place. "Guess the blizzard's really over."

There was a wistful quality to his words. Justice reached a hand across the table to cover his. "We'll all be okay."

"I want to believe you. You know I believe in you but . . ." Ian shook his head. "I'm going to go help Tag. We're right outside."

"Okay." Justice watched him tug on his heavy parka and step into the frozen outdoors. He limped to the window in the bedroom and saw his two men studying the sky and scanning the forest that stretched endlessly across the snowy landscape. They spent another five minutes talking before heading back inside. "Things okay?" he asked as they shed their gear.

"Something's up," Tag said. "I smell fire."

"Like fireplace fire?"

Tag rubbed his hands together to warm them. "Like burn down your motherfucking village fire."

Just then, Justice's phone began to ring. "Comms really are back," he said. "It's Devlin."

"Answer it," Ian told him. "I'm going to hang out over on the couch. Listen to music and stare at the monitors. You two talk to him. Let me know what happens."

The phone gave its fifth and sixth ring, and Devlin would never stop calling. It was time for Justice to face the inevitable. Or, in this case, Devlin. "Hey, Devlin," he said casually.

"Don't you 'Hey, Devlin' me. What the fuck, Justice?"

"There was an avalanche and a blizzard. No comms."

"Obviously, that's not an issue now."

"Right." He looked helplessly at Tag, who just shrugged. Mainly because he was hearing a one-sided conversation. Justice motioned for him to give him a few minutes alone and once he did, Justice lowered his voice. "It's been a long week."

"It's about to get even longer—Itor is on their way to you," Devlin said. "And so am I."

Panic alternated with relief. "How long?"

"We're four hours out, and I think Itor's team is right behind us. I'm on the plane. So let's take this opportunity for you to brief me before I goddamned land."

"Affirmative," Justice answered automatically.

"Is Taggart willing to come to ACRO with you?" Devlin asked straight away.

"He is, yes."

"What aren't you sharing?"

A whole lot. "It's complicated."

On the other end of the phone, Devlin sighed. "Always is. But I prefer knowledge over surprises, especially before you bring a possibly unwilling man through the ACRO gates."

"He was unwilling, but now he understands that ACRO's the best place for him. That it's different from Itor."

"But."

Justice mentally crossed his fingers. "Taggart was most recently in Itor's hands."

"Be specific."

"Taggart was . . . tricked into working with Itor. Forced, really. And he was . . . there when we . . . when I . . ."

Fuck. His voice almost broke, but he stopped talking just in time.

"Justice, you still with me?"

Barely. "Yeah, I'm here, Devlin. I won't let you down."

"I know that, son. But I need to know about Taggart. Was he indoctrinated? Did he kill ACRO agents?"

Justice ground his teeth for a long moment before speaking. When he did, he tried to choose his words carefully. Unemotionally. And failed miserably. "And suppose I answer yes to any of that? Does it matter now that he's free of them? Does it matter that he's like my other half—that he is my other half? That I love him?"

"What are you saying, Justice?"

Justice fisted his free hand, the other holding the phone so tightly it shook. "I won't come back to ACRO if he can't. And you know me well enough to realize I'm a man of my words. I'd never do anything to go against ACRO ever, so even if I couldn't work there, I'd still support ACRO causes."

"Slow down," Devlin commanded. "I never said anything about you not being able to bring Taggart back here with you. I do, however, need to know what we're up against—if he needs counseling or solitary time . . . or if Itor still has a hold on him."

And they were to the next part of this equation, much faster than Justice had anticipated. He glanced toward the other room where Ian sat on the couch, listening to music though his headphones. Tag caught his eye, and he motioned for him to come over.

With one last check on Ian, Justice put the phone on speaker. "Devlin, Taggart's here with us now, okay? Because I'd like you to hear this from both of us."

"I'm listening."

And beginning to lose patience, no doubt. But Justice forged ahead. "We know that Itor's definitely after him. They actually hired a mercenary to come find him."

"Tell me you captured him as well," Devlin demanded.

Justice glanced at Tag, then Ian. *He definitely captured us . . .* "It's not like that, Devlin. Taggart and this merc have a history."

Devlin practically growled on the other end of the phone.

Taggart began to talk. "Devlin, it's Taggart here. I realize what this sounds like. This man—this mercenary—was the one who originally brought me into Itor. But he tried to talk them out of it—he knew I wasn't right for them, but they ignored his wishes."

"When did he tell you that?"

"When he came here, to my cabin, to warn me about Itor. He was rehired by them to find me, and he took the job to keep them off my tail."

"Or lead you—and my agent—right back to them."

And yes, when you looked at it like that, the way he himself had that first day, it sounded perfectly rational. But nothing about this newfound threesome with Tag and Ian was rational. It was all heart, which was, unfortunately, the hardest thing to explain. So he skipped explanation and jumped straight to outcome. "We want to bring him in with us. He wants to come to ACRO."

"For what reason? Immunity?"

"He wants to be with us," Taggart said in no uncertain terms. "And we want to be with him."

"Really? Is that true, Justice?" Devlin asked, fire in his tone.

Taggart gave Justice an *I'm sorry* look, but hell, it was going to come out sooner than later. "It's true. I never thought it would be. Honestly. But I believe him. We've been here for days, waiting out the blizzard, and he's only helped. He could have drugged us and taken us prisoner, could have killed us in our sleep. Hell, when I was hurt, he could have ended me and Tag would never have known I didn't die of a brain bleed. Whatever he's doing—"

"Is probably trying to get inside ACRO, any way he can. Even if it means using gullible boys to do so."

"He's not a boy—neither am I, you asshole," Taggart spat at the phone.

Justice thought his head would probably explode just about now.

"I want this merc's name," Devlin told them. "And don't even think of covering for him by withholding that. Your best shot—your only shot—in all of this is to tell me who he is and let me decide some things. Last time I checked, this was still my agency."

"Yes, Devlin," Justice agreed. It was the fairest way, and so he told Devlin. And that's when the fireworks really began.

From the moment Ian overheard Devlin O'Malley yell, "I want this merc's name," through the phone at Justice, he figured he was a dead man. He managed to keep his composure—and to continue pretending to listen to music—well aware he had two sets of eyes on him. As an Excedo, all his senses were more than average, but hell, Justice hadn't bothered to be at all secretive about his phone call.

Which made Ian want to go to the guy and kiss him. Because . . . fuck, Justice really did trust him. As did Taggart, judging by the way they were telling off the head of ACRO for him.

No one had ever trusted him—not like this, or on any level. Least of all his own family. So whatever he'd done to deserve this, he felt as if it might never be enough.

Now, as he moved his foot to the imaginary beat of his iPod, Justice haltingly revealed his name, and then he held his breath as he waited for the inevitable response.

"Ian Bridges is a merc Seducer, Justice." Devlin's voice rang out, and although he started out controlled, his tone got angry as he went on. "His father was one of the worst. The records on that man—you wouldn't believe the things he's done to young specials. Ian learned from the best. And while his father boasted bringing in well over a hundred specials—and that doesn't include the time he spent working on Itor and ACRO agents—Ian's already brought in well over that in a much shorter span."

Ian wished he couldn't fucking hear. He didn't need Devlin to tell him what he already knew, that he wasn't good for anyone or anything. From a mercenary family who would sell their own mother for a buck.

He wanted to punch something. To run. Because the humiliation ran hot over him. How long could Tag and Justice actually believe in him when they had an authority like Devlin telling them differently?

You knew it would go like this.

And even so, he'd held on to a small sliver of hope, the thing that had been practically beaten out of him. Devlin's words still burned, no matter how expected.

Ian had been on the outside for so long, it was hard to imagine being in anyone's trusted inner circle. Hell, he hadn't even had a trusted inner circle of his own until these two men had barreled into his life and fucked him up good.

He'd never been happier. It was the only reason he'd allow himself to be miserable for the rest of his days, however long they'd be. There were enough bounties on his head for him to know it wouldn't take much longer.

Maybe he should let ACRO arrest him. He could be in jail with Tag—and Justice—close. Or maybe he should just let them be together, the way they were probably meant to be.

Or maybe he needed to find a way to prove himself to Devlin, whatever it took.

CHAPTER 16

W hen Justice hung up with Devlin, he immediately called out, "Ian, I know you fucking heard everything."

Busted. Ian yanked out the earphones, which had seemed too heavy against his ears. God, he needed to stop feeling like crap. Maybe he was coming down with the flu. Some sort of bumfuck Alaska moose flu. "How did you know that?"

"You might be a brilliant Seducer, but you suck at spying." Justice rubbed Tag's cheek with his knuckles, then urged him into the living room with Ian. Ian knew that Tag was as upset as he was—okay, more so, because that hadn't been a best first conversation with Devlin.

"So what now?" Tag asked Justice.

"What now is you both get your shit together," Justice ordered.

In anticipation of his order, Ian was already shoving supplies into his rucksack. Any other time, the inherent command in Justice's voice would've had him naked and on his knees.

But not today. Not now, especially. Not when the men he'd fast been considering 'his' were in danger. Because of him. "Justice—"

"No. We're not discussing this now. You're coming with us. Devlin will put both you and Tag in a safe location while we take down Itor—"

"I'm fighting too, dammit," Taggart growled.

Justice ignored him for the moment. "Let's get our supplies together. Prepare for the worst, okay? In case Itor somehow gets here faster."

"Agreed." Ian was up, helping Justice lay out the ammo they had. Taggart went to the closet full of guns and ammo and began checking supplies there. And there was silence—tense as hell silence—for ten minutes, until Ian couldn't fake it any longer.

"Justice . . . Taggart . . . what if I can't go with you to ACRO? What if your boss wants me dead or—" He cut off as Justice appeared suddenly at his side. "You sure you're not part Excedo?" Ian tried to joke, but Justice had a hand on his chin, forcing him to meet his gaze.

Tag was rubbing his shoulders as Justice told him, "Ian, there's no way we're letting anything happen to you. We'll talk to Devlin . . ."

"And we'll make him bring you on," Taggart added. "He just needs to meet you. To see us together."

"Well, not like in bed together," Justice joked, and it eased some of the tension currently threatening to squeeze Ian's brain out of his ears.

Ian broke a smile. "I know you'll both try. I believe you. I trust you."

"And you don't trust easily," Tag said quietly. "Ian, if Devlin won't accept you . . ." Tag trailed off, and Justice picked up, "Then we'll figure out something."

"We're smart," Taggart added. "Justice and I know a little something about living off the grid."

"But you shouldn't have to," Ian said fiercely.

"No one ever said life was fair," Justice pointed out. "Besides, we've got you now. And we've found each other. It's a trade I'd willingly make."

Taggart reached out to touch both men's shoulders. "Me too."

Ian nodded, too overcome by emotion to trust his words.

Justice, Ian, and Taggart spent the next four hours preparing for a battle. Damned good thing Tag was set up for an apocalypse. They had enough weapons and medical supplies to outfit an army, but Justice really hoped they would never have to break into the two-year supply of MREs.

Because yuck.

A beep on his cell phone alerted him to Dev's arrival, and he quickly hit the deactivation switches on Tag's traps and alarms.

Now it was only a matter of time before all hell broke loose.

Tag looked tense as hell, like he was ready to break apart—or break someone—and neither one was a great option. "What about Ian?"

"What about me?" Ian was in the doorway, having just showered. He was pulling on a shirt, his hair spiky and still a bit wet, and his feet were bare.

Justice pointed toward the door, and Ian raised his brows. "ACRO?"

Tag walked toward him, stood next to him protectively, and drew his weapon. "I won't let them touch you."

"Tag, Jesus, let's not start out that way." Justice went to let in Dev and the team he'd brought—guys he typically didn't work with—before they broke the door down. ACRO could be subtle if necessary, but Devlin didn't believe in subtle much.

He opened it when Devlin was almost there, flanked by men in Arctic camo and stark-white combat gear that blended in with the snow. As soon as they came in, Justice reset the alarms, and Devlin nodded approvingly.

"I've got two dozen agents in position outside the lethal trap zone," Dev said as he took in the small space. Ender, another Excedo with super speed, shoved his ski mask on top of his head and stepped up next to Dev. "Where's Ian?"

Justice looked around to the spot where Ian had just been standing.

Tag gestured to the bedroom. "He's waiting in there."

Devlin motioned to two of his men, and Taggart stepped in front of them when they tried to head that way. "Where the hell are you two going?"

"Taggart, I'm guessing?" Devlin asked. Tag nodded, and Devlin's expression softened slightly. "Listen, I'm taking him into custody."

"He wants to fight," Tag insisted.

"I'm sure he does, but until I know what he's really all about, he's no help to us. To me." Devlin looked to Justice to be the voice of reason.

"What are you going to do with him?" Justice asked.

"Make sure he doesn't run."

"He won't, Devlin."

"I need to make sure that you are safe. You and my men are my priority. And if you both fight me, Taggart's going to be in the cellar with Ian." Fuck, the guy was scarier when he was quiet-pissed.

"It's fine, Taggart." Ian had come to the doorway. He glanced at Justice and nodded, and then said, "I understand, Devlin. I'm not going to make any trouble. I don't want either of these men hurt on my account." He gestured to the trap door in the living room floor. "The basement's secure. I can wait there."

With that, Ian moved to the center of the hallway and the ACRO men flanked him, ushering him through the living room and into the basement.

Dev stared at Ian, but his words were for Justice and Tag. "You're both putting a great deal of faith in a man who no doubt led Itor here."

Tag jumped right in. "No, he didn't. Not intentionally. He had a chip implant that would've activated a homing signal if I hadn't destroyed it." Devlin glanced at Ender and then back at Justice, and Tag spoke again, this time through gritted teeth. "What? I know that look, even if I don't know you at all."

Dev calmly removed his stocking cap, revealing a messy mop of brown hair. "Do you know what the device is called? What model of chip?"

"P-128S," Tag said in a clipped voice. "Why?"

Dev's expression turned grim, and Justice's gut did a slow roll. "That chip is experimental," he said. "Itor uses it in a few different ways. It tracks when it activates, and it explodes if someone tries to take out it. They can also detonate it remotely. It's a nasty weapon. How did you destroy it?"

"I melted it," Tag said.

Devlin gave a slow nod that, to an outsider, would appear neutral. But Justice had seen a flash of . . . something . . . in Dev's dark eyes. Something that said he knew more than he was saying. "So Ian let you destroy it for him? After you discovered it?"

Justice felt his face flush. "We *didn't* discover it," he muttered.

"*Ian* told us about it." Tag folded his arms across his chest as if daring Devlin to challenge him on their version of events. "He didn't have to, but he did. And he's the one who insisted I destroy it."

"He didn't want the chip to activate and lead Itor here," Justice added. "They didn't find out about Tag's cabin from him."

"You really believe that?"

"He's not the same guy he might've been, Devlin. I actually don't think he was ever that guy. His father? He sounds like a real piece of work," Justice admitted.

And then Tag broke in. "This is bullshit. Come on, Devlin—if I hadn't given you my coordinates, could you and your best and brightest at ACRO have found this place?"

Devlin stared, and Justice watched Tag fight the urge to squirm. "With enough time and the right people doing the digging, yeah, we could."

"Well, there you go. If you can, Itor can."

"You know we're here to help you, right? You might try showing a little gratitude."

Tag clenched his teeth, and Justice prayed he'd play nice. The goal here was to keep Ian safe, and Tag wouldn't risk blowing that.

"You're right," he said, grudgingly. "I'm grateful. And I know you have to protect your people. Like I have to protect mine."

Devlin inclined his head. "Then we're on the same page. Just different sides of it."

"Great," Tag said. "Now, let's talk about getting Ian out of the basement—"

Abruptly, Dev looked up, his brown eyes going glassy, the way Justice had seen it happen when his psychic ability kicked in. "No time. They're here," he said. "Itor's on the doorstep."

CHAPTER 17

J ustice and Tag rushed with Dev into the night, where the icy air bitch-slapped them all. Itor was crazy. Who wanted to fight in this shit?

All around them, the forest was alive with motion as ACRO agents slipped into battle-ready positions. Ignoring the ache in his injured leg, Justice stayed on Dev's heels, with Tag pulling up the rear, but before they'd made it ten yards through the deep snow, Tag brushed past Justice and grabbed Dev's parka to swing him around.

"I need to go to Ian," he said. "We can't leave him alone—"

"We need you more than Ian does," Dev said, his voice edged with rare sympathy, especially considering Tag's blatant belligerence. "You'll be back with him soon."

Tag didn't look convinced. In fact, he looked agitated, his nostrils flaring and his jaw tight, and suddenly, Justice felt like a dolt. Quickly, he pulled Tag aside as Dev barked out some orders to two nearby guys.

"Is this about fighting?" A blast of wind stung Justice's eyes, and he slipped on his snow goggles. "Are you going to be able to use your powers? I know how you feel about that."

Tag closed his eyes, for a moment, Justice's heart sank. But when Tag lifted his lids, the determination glinting in those dark eyes erased every bit of Justice's doubt.

"I'm going to tear them apart, Justice." Tag's deep voice became even lower, smoky, as if it had been dragged from out of the pits of Hell. "They're going to pay for every drop of pain they caused Ian, me, you, and our mothers."

All right, then. Justice almost felt a little sorry for anyone stupid enough to be fighting for Itor.

Almost.

Meeting Tag's angry gaze, Justice gave him a reassuring nod, a silent *Let's do this thing*, just the way they'd done when they were kids, play-fighting in the woods near their houses.

Tag nodded back, and then Ender and two guys Justice only knew from seeing them around ACRO's massive grounds guided them along the tree line.

Ender's voice was grave as he spoke to Devlin. "There are more Itor bastards than we anticipated," he growled. "They dropped from a fucking cargo plane and are coming in two waves. Second on snowmobiles."

They eased behind a huge fallen log propped on a rock face, providing excellent shelter from both the wind and Itor bullets.

"Justice, Tag," Dev said. "You two stay with me when the first wave hits. You're more useful here than out there when the second wave comes."

"Yes, sir," Justice said. Tag ground his teeth, but at least he didn't call Dev an asshole.

It was dark out, but the glowing full moon and undulating ribbon of illumination from the aurora borealis provided just enough light to see. Not that Dev needed light—he read situations like this because he was a precog. He'd once explained to Justice that he could actually see what was about to happen, like it was on a TV screen in front of him. So even during the years when Devlin had been blind, he'd been able to guide himself using his second-sight vision—he called it remote viewing—that way.

Suddenly, the sound of a chopper broke the stillness. Two seconds later, the forest exploded with noise—gunfire, shouts, screams. Justice spotted a figure to the right, went down on one knee, and took the bastard out with three shots, center mass.

A brilliant explosion and a flash of heat blasted them backward. Justice slammed into something hard behind him . . . a tree? Didn't matter. The helo above was dropping fucking bombs on them.

The thing banked hard, and Justice's gut dropped into his snow boots. The chopper was loaded heavy with missiles.

And they were aimed at the cabin.

Well, this wasn't unexpected at all.

The two ACRO agents who'd brought Ian into the cellar, where there was no other door or window to the outside, had put him in chains made especially for strong Excedos.

Which meant he wasn't getting out of them anytime soon. But even though he probably could've run rings around these men, he didn't.

He'd suck it the fuck up and be respectful.

To a point. The ever-present headache was starting to intensify, which meant that his patience was very soon going to be very limited.

He glanced between the two agents. "Do you have enough men to fight Itor?"

One of the ACRO agents—a guy named Gus—smirked. "You going to help us fight, Itor-boy?"

"Go fuck yourself. And I don't work for Itor."

"Anymore, right?" Gus asked. "That's what they all say."

"I'm sure," Ian muttered.

And then it got quiet upstairs, the kind of silence that made Ian wary. He stood slowly, not wanting the chains to make noise or to freak out the ACRO agents, and he noticed they'd gone completely still. And all three of them were staring up at the cellar door like they were expecting the end of the world.

And fuck, Ian hated it that Taggart and Justice were up there. They were capable. He knew that. But his protective nature had kicked into high gear. To not be able to actively help his men . . . "This is the worst part."

Gus glanced at him with a frown but didn't say anything. Then all hell broke loose above them.

This was a clusterfuck.

Thick smoke choked the air, the ground shook, and the deafening noises left Justice disoriented and scrambling to stay on his feet. "Tag! The helo!" Somehow he managed to yell despite the fact that his heart was lodged in his throat.

"I'll heat it up!" Tag yelled back from where he was crouched on the ground. He looked up, his eyes focused on the chopper. "Justice, don't let it gain altitude!"

Bracing one hand against a tree for support, Justice engaged his magnetic gift. Power skittered over his skin, an electric tingle that began in his fingertips and spread to his toes and scalp. Gaze fixed on the helicopter's black belly, he pictured himself taking the entire machine in his fist and dragging it toward him.

The bird pitched hard as the pilot attempted to compensate for the sudden force that was trying to reel it in. A searing, agonizing tugging sensation wrapped around Justice's rib cage, cutting off his breath and driving him to his knees.

"I can't . . . hold it . . . for long."

"Hold on, buddy . . . Hold . . . on." Tag's voice was strained as he focused on the helo, his body trembling, his panting breaths freezing in the air.

The helicopter pitched again, but then it rolled, bucking like a bull trying to throw its rider. But the glow of hot metal spreading toward the gas tank was about to end all of that—

"Take cover!" Tag yelled.

Justice didn't hesitate. He hit Tag in a tackle and took him to the snow as the massive boom shattered the air. The ground rumbled, heat scorched them, and bits of debris rained down, punching through the deep snow. Steam rose up from the blackened snow craters, the hiss of hot metal the only sound in the stunned forest.

A shot rang out, and it was on again.

Beneath Justice, Tag cursed and spit snow. "I could have hit the ground all by myself, you know," he muttered.

"That's no fun." He gave Tag a discreet—and hard—pinch on the ass as he pushed off the other man. He didn't wait around to flirt; Itor agents on snowmobiles were tearing up the forest, some of the riders firing weapons, while others *were* weapons.

One hurled a fireball at an ACRO agent who barely avoided being toasted by engaging his super speed, and another was wielding some sort of electrical whips extending from the tips of his fingers.

"Bastards," Justice growled. Throwing out his hand, he sent his own gift at the electric-whip guy's snowmobile as it sped toward the cabin's clearing. The thing veered hard to the right and collided with a tree. At the same time, another snowmobile crashed, and Justice looked over to see Tag with a self-satisfied smirk.

They joined forces, working in tandem to take out more snowmobiles and riders as the other ACRO agents engaged Itor.

For fun, Justice sent one snowmobile into a collision with an Itor agent, and then he and Tag crashed two head-on.

"It's like a fucking video game," Justice yelled at Tag.

Grinning, Tag flicked his wrist, and the last snowmobile flipped into the air, dumping its driver in a heap in the snow. ACRO agents swarmed the guy, and soon he joined a handful of other Itor survivors in restraints near the shed.

Eventually, only a few lone shots rang out, punctuated by groans and shouts for help from the injured and dying. Justice and Tag helped round everyone up, bringing them inside the cabin, where uninjured ACRO agents with medical experience tended to the wounded.

"Ian is a trained medic." Tag grabbed Dev's arm, and Justice groaned. Tag was going to push the guy too far, and probably sooner than later. "Did you hear me, dammit? He's a medic. He can help."

For a long time, Dev stared at Tag, measuring him from head to toe.

"Dev," Justice pleaded, fighting the adrenaline that rushed through his body from the fighting and subsequent victory. "Please. He deserves a chance to prove himself."

Dev jerked his chin at the basement hatch. "Go. And good job tonight."

Yeah. Good job. Justice should be thrilled. They'd defeated the bad guys, and while there were a lot of injured men being cared for in the cabin or being evacced immediately in the most critical cases, there were no casualties. At least, not on ACRO's side. But something niggled at him. The expression on Dev's face earlier, when they'd been discussing Ian . . . Justice would bet his left nut that his boss was keeping something from them.

So yep, they'd won the battle. But he had a feeling the fight was not yet over.

CHAPTER 18

The quieter of the two ACRO agents babysitting Ian checked his phone and looked over at his buddy, Gus. "Devlin needs me. Hang here with him."

"Great."

"It's no picnic for me either," Ian said brightly as the agent raced up the stairs and slammed through the doorway. His humor fled though, as fear for Justice and Tag settled into the pit of his stomach. "Care to share what's happening?"

Before Gus could reply, Justice's voice drifted down the stairs, and Ian nearly sagged with relief. "Dev said to let Ian up—we need a medic!"

"Now, asshole," Tag shouted, and Ian snorted. So Tag.

Gus frowned, but he checked his phone and must've gotten the confirmation he needed because he reached into his coat pocket and pulled out a key. "Don't fuck this up."

"I don't plan on it." Ian watched him unlock one cuff, and then they both froze as a boom rattled the shelves and rows of supplies stacked along the walls, sending cans of soup and bottles of water crashing to the floor.

"What the fu—" Gus cut off as the wall in front of them exploded outward.

Wood, stone, and dust pelted them, but the real danger was the Itor agent who crashed through the opening. In an instant, Justice was looking down the barrel of a pistol.

Son of a bitch!

The bastard fired even as Ian shoved Gus down and moved out of the way himself, encumbered by the chains but free enough to put on a burst of speed and avoid a bullet to the brain. Out of the corner of his eye, he saw movement through the wall opening the trigger-happy Itor dick had emerged from, and shit, more agents were storming through what appeared to be an ancient, narrow tunnel.

Tag, you should have studied the damned building plans.

Two more agents burst in and Gus was up, rushing to fight the first one. Real quick, it became obvious that Gus was an Excedo—with a single punch to the chest, he knocked the agent into the back wall hard enough to displace a section of stonework and likely kill the guy.

Ian didn't have time to celebrate. One of the newcomers came at him, the sleeves of his jacket peeled back enough to reveal his secret weapon: venomous barbs.

Not. Good.

Heart pounding, Ian hurled himself at the guy and used the chain still connected to his wrist as a weapon. With an angry shout, he wrapped it around the guy's neck before he could shoot off venom from his barbs. The barbed agent grunted as Ian yanked the chain to cut off his air. The Itor bastard struggled hard, one hand going for the chain at his throat, the other flailing wildly behind him as he tried to stick Ian with the tip of his poison barb.

Holy shit, was this idiot ever going to go down?

"Help . . ." Gus's voice was a tortured whisper from behind him. Ian cranked his head around to see the ACRO agent standing, unnaturally still, near the staircase, his eyes wide with panic.

The remaining Itor guy was stalking toward him, knife in hand, but his real weapon was the hypnotic ability he was using to hold Gus immobile.

Summoning every last drop of strength he had, Ian slammed poison-boy to the ground hard enough that he was never getting up and charged the hypnotist. Speed was his blessing in this case—he moved too fast for the guy to get a bead on him, but for some reason, for all his speed, he suddenly felt like he was moving in slow motion. Still, his slow motion was twice as fast as a normal human, and he managed not only to disarm the enemy, but to slice his neck open with his own damned knife. Fucking satisfying as hell.

Straightening, he winced at the throb in his head. Damn this headache. At least none of the Itor agents were moving. Gus was blinking, rubbing his eyes, and as Ian helped him up, he could sympathize. Ian's own eyes were stinging, his vision blurring, and what the hell was going on?

He stumbled, felt his legs go wobbly.

"Ian, what's wrong?" Gus's voice sounded far away.

Ian glanced at the barbed Itor guy. Looked down at himself. Had he been jabbed by one of the poisonous spurs without noticing? He'd been so fucking careful, but, what if . . .

Pain tore through him—searing, stinging agony, as if a million fire ants were biting at him from the inside. His pulse pounded in his ears, deafening him. At some point, everything went black and then, blissfully, there was nothing at all.

"Ian's down!"

Justice heard those terrifying words as he and Tag were trying to wrench the basement door open. The explosion from below had twisted the hinges, and holy shit, all Justice could think about was Ian. Finally, with Dev's help, they managed to rip the door loose.

Tag ended up in front of him as they took the now-wobbly stairs two at a time and dropped into chaos. Justice's heart raced at the sight of the collapsed wall and bodies littering the floor, but then his ticker skidded to a halt when he saw Gus hunched over Ian's motionless body, his hands probing for injuries.

No. Oh . . . no.

Tag hit the floor next to Ian with a crack of kneecaps. "What happened?" he barked, his words thick with emotion, and Justice was just glad that he'd been the one to ask that question, because he didn't think he could speak at all past the lump in his throat.

"He saved my ass," Gus said roughly. "Then he collapsed. That Itor guy next to the shelves—he's got those venomous barbs."

"Shit." Devlin was behind them. Working quickly, he crossed to the dead guy and snapped a picture of the exposed barbs with his phone.

Justice's mouth went dry as he looked down at Ian, his pale skin covered in sweat. He was unconscious, but each wheezy breath sounded labored, as if even in his passed-out state he was trying to claw his way back to the living.

"It's okay," Justice said, his voice humiliatingly hoarse as he joined Tag next to Ian. "We're here."

Ian's eyes popped open, and Justice exhaled with relief. Until he saw the pain and fear glazing them.

Tag gripped Ian's hand so tightly that his knuckles turned white. "You hold on. We're getting an antidote." He glanced over at Justice, his eyes pleading. "Right?"

Justice could only nod. He knew that there were different types of venom in the barbs, and some had antidotes . . .

Most didn't. He held his breath waiting for Devlin to get the answer from ACRO—Justice knew that's who he'd sent the picture back to. There were scientists on call 24-7, just for emergencies like this one. And Devlin's teams traveled with whatever antidotes they could produce but . . .

Time slowed to a crawl as he counted each rise and fall of Ian's chest. There was activity all around him, but he barely noticed. At some point, Gus had gotten up to gather medical supplies, but where the hell were ACRO's crack scientists with the damned info they needed?

"Don't we have anything to give him?" Tag's raspy voice brought Justice out of his own head. Ian had closed his eyes, was still breathing hard. Gus appeared with an oxygen tank and mask, and as Justice helped place it over Ian's mouth, Tag gripped his wrist. "Justice, please. Give him something."

"If we give him the wrong antidote . . ." He couldn't finish, but Tag got it quickly enough.

"But we have antidotes for every kind of venom, right?"

Dammit. Tag knew the answer to that as well as he did. He was looking for a reassurance, and Justice was willing Dev to give him one. He'd probably settle for a lie at this point, but that wasn't going to help save Ian . . .

Ian, who was ripping the mask off. Justice tried to force it on him, but the guy was still strong. "No," he managed. "Please."

"Ian," Tag begged, "put the mask on until we figure out what to do."

Ian grabbed for Tag, pulled Justice closer too. "Thank you."

"Jesus, Ian— Don't you fucking dare!" He hadn't meant to yell, but he was back, cradling his mom's head while she died in his arms. And Tag had begged him to help then, too.

It was the one thing Justice felt he could never, ever make up to Tag. And he couldn't lose Ian, not after finding something this goddamned special in the middle of hell.

Devlin was kneeling down now. Justice didn't even have to look at him to know the answer—he could feel it coming off Devlin in waves.

"I'm sorry," Devlin said quietly.

"You fix this," Tag told him. "It's your fucking fault he was down here. He could've been up with us. We would've kept him safe."

Devlin stared at Tag—he'd never kick a man when he was down like this, Justice knew. Devlin shouldered blame better than anyone.

"I don't know how the barb got him," Gus said. "Ian was so fucking fast—even with the chain. I could barely see him."

"Ah, shit," Dev muttered. "Of course."

Justice whipped his head around to Dev. "Of course . . . what?"

Dev met Justice's gaze. "His chip. It could be killing him."

"Killing him?" Justice shook his head. "We told you—"

"If you were right about the model of the chip, it was loaded with both an explosive and a toxin. Tag might have destroyed the explosive element, but it's possible that he inadvertently caused the poison to leak before the chip melted."

Tag exploded to his feet, fists clenched, and Justice got ready to . . . to what? Intervene? He was as angry and blindsided as Tag was. Now he knew why Dev had seemed to be holding back something when they discussed the chip.

"Are you *fucking* kidding me?" Tag practically hurled the words at Dev. "The chip is full of poison, and you just *now* thought to tell us about it?"

"It didn't seem relevant at the time," Devlin said evenly, not giving in to Tag's anger. "Ian didn't appear to be ill, so there was no reason to alarm anyone." An edge of warning deepened his voice as his patience with Tag began to wear thin. "Especially not when we were about to be fighting for our lives."

"Dammit." Frustrated with his inability to help and terrified for Ian, Justice shoved a hand through his hair. "You made a good call, isn't that right, Tag?" Tag gave a reluctant nod, and he continued. "But what now? If the chip did this, what kind of poison is it?"

"Hold on." Devlin's long fingers flew over his phone's keyboard, texting, no doubt, to the scientists. "They say it's most likely either a hematological or neurological toxin." He frowned at the screen. "Maybe both. Whatever it is, it'll have some sort of mineral base, and it'll—"

"Wait." Tag broke in. "Did you say mineral? What kind of mineral?"

"Does it matter?"

"It matters, Devlin," Justice assured him.

There were a few seconds of silence and then Devlin read, "Pyrrhotite." He glanced up. "But the pyrrhotite is just the vehicle for the poison. If my guys are right, they bonded the poison to the lodestone, and the molecules have been carrying the poison to all his organs and nervous system, including his brain, since the moment the chip was destroyed. There's no way to get it out of him."

"Yes, there is." Justice grinned. "Most pyrrhotite is magnetic."

Tag locked gazes with him, the hope in his eyes drawing Justice as if *that* was Tag's power. "Pyrrhotite contains iron. We'll have to lock hard on its signature or we'll pull out the necessary iron in his body."

"You'll also have to keep it contained once it's outside his body so it won't spread through the air," Dev added.

Shit, this wasn't going to be easy. The worry must have shown on his face, because Dev clapped a hand on his shoulder. "You can do this. You're never stronger than when you're fighting for someone's life."

"He's right, Justice." Tag went down on heels and stroked his hand over Ian's head as he looked up at Justice. "I've never seen anyone who fights harder." His throat worked on a swallow. "Now we'll fight together."

In any other situation, he'd have kissed Tag until they both combusted, but right now, they had to make sure Ian was there to share the heat.

"Our magnetic powers kick some serious ass," Justice said. "So let's do this."

Dev gave a nod, but Justice had already summoned his power, and next to him, the air pulsed with the magnetic energy radiating from Tag. In a moment, they'd start pushing each other apart unless they either concentrated their power on a metal object or Justice reversed his power . . . and then they'd snap together so hard they'd crack their skulls.

They'd tried it a few times as kids, and it'd always ended badly.

By mutual, unspoken consent that came as naturally as it had for so many years, Justice rolled Ian onto his side, and Tag yanked up Ian's shirt. Ian groaned as Devlin and Gus kneeled to hold him steady. He'd gone ashen, and his breathing was getting choppier. Shallower.

"Shit," Justice breathed. "We gotta do this fast."

"Let's go." Tag took one of Justice's hands in his, their fingers twining with familiarity. Gently, they each laid their free hands on the cool, clammy skin of Ian's back. "Now."

Justice turned on his power full blast, focusing it into the palm of his hand. Energy sang through him, vibrating his body, his bones, his very cells. Tag might as well have been a nuclear power plant, his energy buzzing against Justice's in the air between them.

There . . . he could feel the metals in Ian's body quiver—all the metals. Closing his eyes, he felt around for the special "feel" of pyrrhotite, it's unique molecular structure allowing him to pick it apart from all other metals and minerals. He focused on iron, and then began what seemed like a way-too-slow process of locating only the right iron sulfide molecular combination. He knew Tag was doing the same, and . . . there! He focused on the signature, and instantly, the pyrrhotite that had spread through Ian's body began to move toward Justice's palm.

Suddenly, Ian's spine went stiff, his body convulsing. "Hold him down!" he shouted. Or, at least, tried to shout. His voice was hoarse with the effort required to draw the mineral out of Ian's tissues slowly, without damaging anything. Fuck, he'd take yanking a moving helicopter out of the sky over this any day.

"It's happening," Tag ground out, his hand clutching Justice's in a fierce grip.

They hadn't worked together like this in years, but sleeping together the last few days, touching one another constantly, had been like a shortcut for this moment. Justice squeezed Tag's hand just as hard and concentrated on the thick, quicksilver fluid he could picture in his mind's eye.

Come on, come on, comeoncomeoncomeon . . .

Slowly—so fucking slowly—he could feel the pyrrhotite near the surface of Ian's skin.

"Almost," he said between panting breaths. "Almost . . ."

He felt the mineral push through Ian's flesh before he saw it, the dusty particles forming an almost sugary coating on his skin.

"I didn't know it was crystalline," Dev murmured, his voice deep with awe.

"That's . . . the . . . poison," Justice managed.

The mineral dust vibrated as it came free of Ian's body and floated up to stick to Justice's and Tag's palms. When the last particle finally popped out of Ian's body, he relaxed, but only a little.

"Get soap and a bowl of hot water," Tag rasped. "We need to wash off the poison before we release our power, or it'll get into the air."

Gus flew up the stairs, leaving Dev to ease Ian onto his back while Justice and Tag kept the poison dust firmly in their hands with their powers. "He's already looking better," he said, and yeah, Ian's color was coming back, and his breathing had evened out.

Gus returned with two bowls, one for washing and the other for rinsing, and Tag and Justice wasted no time in washing the shit off. The moment their hands were free of the rinse water, both Justice and Tag released their power and fell forward as if their bones had turned to Jell-O.

Justice had broken out in a sweat—Tag had too, making their hands slippery. But now he knew neither man would ever let go again. Not in the ways that mattered, anyway.

They lay like that for a long time, draped partly over Ian and partly over each other, until he felt himself being lifted and Devlin's hand on the back of his neck. A soft rub, a quiet, "Justice, come on, wake up," and he opened his eyes, feeling drained and woozy. Across from him, Gus was holding Tag up.

Justice cut his gaze to Ian, still on the floor and covered in sweat, but with his eyes open, the hint of a smile on his face, looking between him and Tag.

They'd done it. Together. If all the pieces hadn't fit together before this . . .

He heard his mom's last whispered words inside his head. *Sometimes, things are left to fate, Justice. You can't fight fate. You simply have to let fate take care of you.*

CHAPTER 19

J ustice and Ian were still asleep. At some point during the night, Tag had gotten up to stretch out on the couch and get some real shut-eye. His queen-sized mattress was fine for three men fucking or two men sleeping, but three men sleeping was definitely a crowd.

Tag slipped into his snow gear and stepped outside into a beautiful day. Yes, it was still dark, but a fresh layer of snow coated everything, wiping out the signs of battle from the day before and turning the place into a Christmas dream.

It was also thirty below, and he was going to freeze if he didn't hurry.

Quickly, he grabbed the ax from the shed and snowshoed about thirty yards away, to the tree he knew wanted to come home with him. Somehow it had survived being shredded by bullets or charred by missiles or the helicopter crash, but not everything had been so lucky. Before Dev and his team had finally cleared out, he'd promised to send a crew to clean up.

He'd also formally offered both Tag and Ian a job.

They'd both accepted, and both had given only one condition. Ian had asked that he be sent only on missions that didn't require his seduction skills. Those, he whispered to Justice and Tag, were reserved for them, and them alone.

Tag swung the ax at the base of the tree, bracing himself for the impact. He'd done the same when he'd waited for Dev to reply to his demand. Turned out he hadn't needed to brace for anything. Devlin O'Malley was exactly as Justice had described: firm, but fair.

Tag faced Devlin, but for the first time since the guy had walked through the front door, he faced him with respect, not suspicion. "I don't want to be a field agent."

Justice nodded encouragement from where he stood with Ian near the fridge. Ian saluted with a beer bottle. Which reminded Tag that he could really use a cold one.

Dev cocked his head, and Tag suddenly wondered if the guy could read minds. "Is it because you don't like to use your powers? Because you'd be surprised how many agents come to us with a love/hate relationship with their abilities. We can help."

Tag slid a glance at Ian, and his heart fluttered with warmth. The man was alive right now because of the ability Tag and Justice had used on him. "Actually, I'm pretty much over that." He considered his next words carefully, which was pretty much a first for him. "I did what I had to do tonight, but I don't like to kill. Itor forced me to do it, and I know we're going to have to talk about that eventually. But I'd like some assurance that I can apply my ability to something other than fighting or undercover work."

Dev grinned, and suddenly he could see the man and not the person in charge of the most powerful secret agency in the world. "You have no idea how much we can use you in our sciences department." He paused, his expression going serious but his voice teasing, "After you go through basic training. Something tells me you'll need to go through the class on understanding the chain of command twice."

Tag snorted. But the guy was probably right.

Smiling at the memory, he went back to concentrating on Christmas, and twenty minutes later, he was inside the cabin again, inhaling the aroma of the coffee and cinnamon rolls he'd made before he left. The warmth of the fire thawed him as he used the fireplace poker stand to hold up the tree. He didn't have ornaments, but he did have a leftover length of LED string lights that the cabin's builder had used to illuminate the stairs going down to the now-destroyed basement during an emergency.

It didn't take him long to wrap them around the tree and get them lit up. He took a few more minutes to hide gifts in the branches, and just as he was admiring his work, Ian and Justice emerged from the bedroom, their noses leading them toward the kitchen.

When Justice looked over and saw the tree, he froze.

This was going to be a crapshoot. Until the day their moms died, Justice had loved Christmas. They both had. Their mothers had made sure that even though they didn't exactly have a traditional family structure, they still celebrated like a family. Justice and his mom always stayed over at Tag's house on Christmas Eve, and in the morning, Justice's mom made cinnamon rolls that they scarfed while they opened presents.

So, okay, this wasn't exactly like when they were kids. The tree was kind of pathetic, there were no wrapped presents, and there was no TV to play *A Christmas Story* in the background. And the longer Justice stood there, staring at the tree like it was an enemy in need of being shot, the more Tag worried that this might have been a really bad idea.

"What the hell is that?" Justice asked as Ian poured coffee for the three of them.

Tag wasn't going to play that game. "Remember when we found that scraggly stray cat, Lucky? Remember how he was cold and scared, and we brought him home and nursed him back to health?" Tag gestured to the tree. "It was cold and scared, and I brought it in to warm it up."

"Fuck." Justice scrubbed a hand over his face. "Tag, I told you—"

"I think it's awesome." Ian brought over the coffee and put all three mugs on the coffee table. "And he made cinnamon rolls."

"Of course he did."

Tag bit back a grin at Justice's annoyance. "And there's more." He grabbed the blanket off the couch and spread it out on the floor. "Sit."

Ian shrugged and Justice bitched and moaned, but they obeyed while Tag popped the cork on a bottle of bubbly he'd chilled overnight.

"You're telling me you just happened to have champagne sitting around in your doomsday shelter?" Justice said.

Tag poured the sparkling wine into three plastic cups. Classy. But hey, he hadn't exactly planned on entertaining.

"The previous owner said it's tradition. You keep a bottle of champagne at all times, and you drink it whenever an apocalypse doesn't happen. You know, the Y2K thing, or the Mayan 2012 thing, or whenever some nut-job decides the Bible says the world is going to end on a certain date." He handed them each a cup and sank down onto the blanket with them so they formed a three-person circle. "In a

SYDNEY CROFT

way, we did survive an apocalypse. An avalanche. Itor. Each other." He
held up his cup. "And it's Christmas. We should celebrate."

"Tag—"

He cut off Justice with a hand on his thigh. "Don't. Listen to me.
What happened four years ago . . . it was the worst day of our lives.
It's tied to Christmas, and I understand that. But our mothers would
want us to be happy, and I think we're honoring their memories by
keeping their traditions alive. Christmas is about family. And you two
are my family."

Justice still looked uncertain. But then Ian looked down at his
cup. "I've never had a Christmas," he said. "Family get-togethers
weren't really a thing, you know?"

Tag had known that Ian wasn't big on Christmas, but he'd
never gone into detail. It wasn't that he'd hated it—he'd just seemed
ambivalent about it. Now Tag knew why.

"Listen to me," Tag told them both. "No more bad memories.
From now on, we make new ones."

Justice and Ian exchanged glances. A slow smile turned up Ian's
face, and even Justice's lips twitched tentatively.

"Yeah," Justice said softly. "New memories."

Ian leaned over and kissed Justice. Leaned the other direction and
pressed his firm lips to Tag's. "To new memories," he murmured.

They raised their cups. "To new memories."

Grinning, Tag said, "I didn't have time to shop, what with Itor
playing Grinch, but I do have presents for you."

Justice winced. "I can only imagine."

"It better not be reindeer jerky or bear sausage or some shit," Ian
muttered.

Taggart laughed. "Nope. Better." He set aside his cup and reached
into the tree branches to pull out a short length of coiled rope. "Justice,
this is for you."

For a moment, Justice stared. Damn, this had backfired . . .

"Shit, Tag, just what I wanted." His voice had gone dark and
smoky . . . and when he looked up, so had his eyes.

Instant. Erection.

"Yo, Santa." Ian leaned toward Tag again. "Don't suppose you
have a blindfold for me hidden inside your little Charlie Brown tree?"

Damn, he knew these guys well. Tag produced a long scarf and handed it to Ian. "Merry Christmas. Next year I'll do it right."

Justice shook his head. "*This* year you did it right." Going to his hands and knees, he crawled over to Tag and drew him into a deep, powerful kiss. He felt Ian's hot breath on the back of his neck and his arousal pressing into his spine as they both surrounded him.

This, he thought, was shaping up to be the best Christmas ever.

His mother had always said that Christmas was about family, and somehow, after four years of hell and loneliness, he had one again.

So yeah, best Christmas ever.

Explore more ménage relationships with our other *Share the Love* holiday charity stories:

Dear Reader,

Thank you for reading Sydney Croft's *Three the Hard Way*!

We know your time is precious and you have many, many entertainment options, so it means a lot that you've chosen to spend your time reading. We really hope you enjoyed it.

We'd be honored if you'd consider posting a review—good or bad—on sites like **Amazon, Barnes & Noble, Kobo, Goodreads, Twitter, Facebook, Tumblr,** and your blog or website. We'd also be honored if you told your friends and family about this book. Word of mouth is a book's lifeblood!

For more information on upcoming releases, author interviews, blog tours, contests, giveaways, and more, please sign up for our weekly, spam-free newsletter and visit us around the web:

Newsletter: tinyurl.com/RiptideSignup
Twitter: twitter.com/RiptideBooks
Facebook: facebook.com/RiptidePublishing
Goodreads: tinyurl.com/RiptideOnGoodreads
Tumblr: riptidepublishing.tumblr.com

Thank you so much for Reading the Rainbow!

RiptidePublishing.com

ACKNOWLEDGMENTS

We want to thank all of the readers who have been asking for more Sydney Croft—this is for you! And a big thanks to Riptide Publishing and Sarah Frantz for giving us the opportunity to dive back into the ACRO world!

ALSO by SYDNEY CROFT

Riding the Storm
Unleashing the Storm
Seduced by the Storm
Taming the Fire
Tempting the Fire
Taken by Fire
Hot Nights, Dark Desires
The Mammoth Book of Special Ops Romance

ABOUT *the* AUTHORS

Sydney Croft is the alter ego of Larissa Ione and Stephanie Tyler (who also writes as SE Jakes), two *New York Times* best-selling authors who blend their very different writing interests into adventurous tales of erotic paranormal fiction. Together, they developed a world where people with extraordinary abilities, like the power to control storms, could live and work with others like them. The series has been described as "Erotica meets the X-Men," and is unique in its own "erotic superhero romance" niche.

Larissa and Stephanie live in different states and communicate almost entirely through email, though they often get together for conferences and book signings.

For more information about Stephanie, Larissa, and Sydney Croft, please check out these links!
www.StephanieTyler.com
www.LarissaIone.com
www.SydneyCroft.com

You can also find Larissa and Stephanie on Twitter and Facebook:
@LarissaIone
@StephanieTyler
@authorSEJakes
www.facebook.com/AuthorStephanieTyler
www.facebook.com/OfficialLarissaIone

Enjoy more stories like
Three the Hard Way
at RiptidePublishing.com!

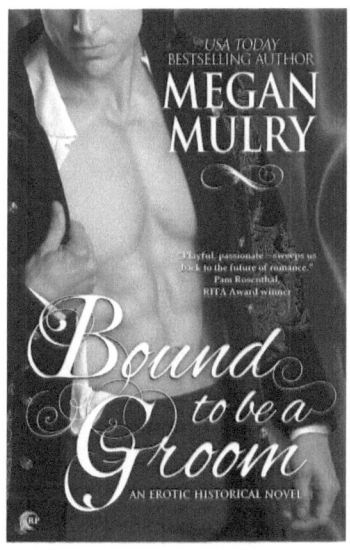
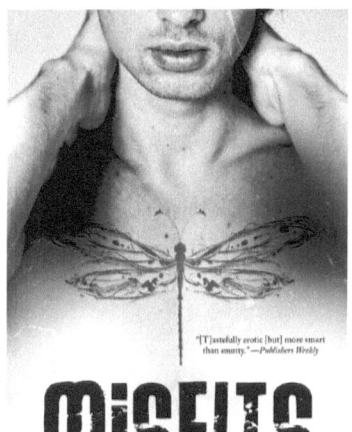